Rose lifted [...]
suggesting th[...]
a partnership [...]
arrangement?"

Edward cleared his throat, and he squirmed nervously. "Well, I would expect it to be a marriage in the full meaning of the word. I would live here, or I could buy another house."

Rose stared at him with reproachful eyes. She swallowed hard, seething with anger and humiliation. Her curt voice lashed at him.

"Of all the arrogant men, you take the prize, Mr. Moody. You're forgetting one important person in this arrangement. Martin! He made it plain last week that he doesn't want anything to do with you, and he hasn't changed his mind. Until he does, I will not be a party to force him to do so."

Sallie entered with the well-filled tea tray, but Rose stopped her with a wave of her hand. She backed out of the room.

"As for marriage, Mr. Moody, if you think for a minute that I'd enter into a union such as you've described, you don't know much about women. I've prayed for years to find a man who loves me and whom I could love. I believe God will answer that prayer in His time. And when He does, I don't want to be tied up in a marriage of convenience."

Rose's voice faltered and tears threatened to overflow, which only increased her anger. She didn't want to cry before this man who had hurt her so badly.

"I'm not for sale, and neither is my son. We are not interested in your proposition. Leave my house and don't ever come back."

IRENE BRAND published her first books in 1984. She became a Barbour author in 1990. By the end of 2006, she will have had forty books published with two others contracted for 2007. Irene lives with her husband, Rod, at Southside, West Virginia. She is active in her local Baptist church, where she teaches Sunday school, plays the piano and/or organ, directs the music program, and serves as the treasurer.

Books by Irene Brand

HEARTSONG PRESENTS
HP9—Heartstrings
HP230—Afterglow
HP515—Love Almost Lost

Where the River Flows

Irene Brand

Heartsong Presents

A note from the Author:
I love to hear from my readers! You may correspond with me by writing:

Irene Brand
Author Relations
PO Box 721
Uhrichsville, OH 44683

ISBN 1-59789-002-2

WHERE THE RIVER FLOWS

All scripture quotations are taken from the King James Version of the Bible.

All of the characters and events in this book are fictitious. Any resemblance to actual persons, living or dead, or to actual events is purely coincidental.

Our mission is to publish and distribute inspirational products offering exceptional value and biblical encouragement to the masses.

PRINTED IN THE U.S.A.

prologue

1876

The last sunbeams of the day turned the water into a blaze of gold as Rose Thurston lifted the gingham dress above her knees and dangled her bare feet in the tranquil Ohio River. In the shallow water of a nearby creek, young frogs' efforts to imitate the croaking of their elders produced nothing except weak, throaty rumbles.

Rose closed her eyes and let the peace of her surroundings seep into her soul and heart. Spring on the Ohio River! Could any other place on earth compare to the peace and joy of living on a shanty boat? But how could she know? Rose couldn't remember any other life.

Rose's birthday was the first day of June, and her grandpa always promised that by that time, their home, the *Vagabond*, would have started its summer voyage. Grandpa Harry hadn't broken his word in her eighteen years. Rose endured the six months their shanty boat was moored at Louisville, looking forward to the rest of the year when she would enjoy the isolation and pleasure of cruising Kentucky's rivers. Two more months to wait. As Gramps often told her, the river was in her blood!

Lottie Thurston finished her evening chores and joined her granddaughter on the rear deck of the *Vagabond*. She brushed back her silvery gray hair and lowered her body into her favorite chair, which squeaked under her weight.

Rocking slowly back and forth, Lottie said, "Peaceful, ain't it."

"But I have a feeling it won't stay that way," Rose said, motioning to the steamboat, *River Belle*, edging close to their river home. Several blasts from the boat's whistle bellowed out a distress signal. The paddlewheel slapped the water softly as the boat slowed down and drifted within a few feet of the shanty.

Rose pulled her feet from the water and ran inside. The waves caused by the towboat swayed the smaller craft, and she held on to a dresser to steady herself as she put on her shoes.

The captain of the *River Belle*, who was well known to the Thurstons, called from the pilothouse.

"I've got a sick woman for you, Lottie."

Rose had rejoined her grandmother on the deck by the time two deckhands lowered a gangplank to make a bridge to the shanty. A small woman, supported by a man, walked timorously across the narrow walkway. She wore a long, gray linen dress with ribbons interwoven on the skirt of the gown. A tiny hat with a narrow brim was perched on her upswept hairdo. The long cloak she wore didn't hide the fact that she was in the family way.

"When your wife is ready to travel, you can hail another packet boat," the captain called to his unloading passengers.

If the brawny man heard the captain, he didn't reply. He was dressed in a black waistcoat, narrow-legged trousers, and a plaid vest. As soon as they reached the safety of the shanty boat, a tortured groan escaped the woman's lips, and she fainted. Her husband caught her before she reached the floor and swung her into his arms. He turned to Lottie, his deep-set brown eyes desperate.

"Are you the midwife? My name is Edward Moody, and this is Martha, my wife. Please, help us."

The woman roused, and her body stiffened in his arms.

"Quick, bring her inside," Lottie said.

Moody ducked his head to clear the low door of the boat.

Lottie quickly spread a heavy quilt over the narrow bed that she and her husband shared. "Lay her here." To Rose, she said, "Bring everything I need while I undress the woman."

"The baby isn't due for two months, or I wouldn't have brought her along," Moody explained.

Lottie started unbuttoning the woman's dress. By the time Rose returned with the ointments and herbs that Lottie used for pain, she had laid the woman's dress aside and was removing her chemise and corset.

The man looked quickly at Rose. "Isn't she too young to be involved?" he asked. "I can help you."

"Children grow up fast on the frontier, Mr. Moody, but she ain't as young as she looks. Rose knows what to do. Go out on the deck and wait. I'll do the best I can for your wife."

The woman on the bed was conscious when Rose brought a bowl of cool water. "I'm all right, Edward," she muttered softly. "Don't worry about me."

"The pains will come in waves," Lottie told her. "Don't try to fight them. Yell if you want to. You'll have time to get your wind before the next one comes."

Rose moistened a clean cloth and started bathing the patient's face. Martha clamped her lips between her teeth, and Rose realized she must be in a great deal of pain. She admired the woman for her courage—not only to start out on a voyage when she was expecting a child, but also her desire to suppress her pain.

Lottie handed Rose the woman's soiled garments, and Rose exchanged an anxious glance with her grandmother. The clothes were soaked with blood. Lottie worked feverishly trying to stanch the flow of blood spreading over the quilt.

Edward Moody had not heeded Lottie's orders to leave the room, and he hovered over the bed. When he saw the blood, he cried, "Do something. She's bleeding to death. Do something!"

"I'm doing all I can, Mr. Moody," Lottie said wearily.

For hours, Martha Moody endured her agony in silence. Finally she screamed, an animal-like sound that raised the hair on the back of Rose's neck and caused cold chills to skitter down her spine. The woman sat upright in the bed as a spurt of bloody fluid gushed from her body, bearing in its wake the immature body of a baby. Lottie grabbed the child, cut the cord, and quickly cleansed some of the clotted blood from the newborn. She turned him upside down and patted his rear. A weak cry escaped the babe's lips. The mother smiled weakly at the sound and slumped on the bed.

"Forget the child," Edward Moody cried, pushing Lottie aside and kneeling by the bed. He pulled his unconscious wife into his arms. "Save my wife. Save my wife! Martha, don't die," he pleaded.

Still working with the baby, Lottie said, "There isn't anything more I can do for your wife. Nobody can lose that much blood and live. I'm sorry."

Moody released his wife and stamped around the small room like a madman, his head clearing the ceiling by less than an inch. "You're sorry!" he shouted. "Is that all you can say? I should have taken her to a doctor instead of letting some quack work on her."

Confronting the man, Rose said, "Don't talk like that to my grandmother! She can't work miracles. Why don't you put the blame where it belongs? You should have stayed at home with your wife instead of bringing her on a river journey in her condition."

"That will do, Rose," Lottie said firmly. "Mr. Moody is hurting enough without you giving him a tongue-lashing." She handed the baby, now wrapped in a scrap of clean blanket, to Rose. "Take him to the kitchen and try to get some sugar water into him."

Rose heated a few teaspoons of sugar and spring water over the coals in the stove. She didn't remember ever holding such a small baby. He looked more like a skinny puppy than a human. "Poor little tyke," she whispered as she dabbed a cloth in the sugar water and held it to his lips. He was very weak, but she succeeded in squeezing some of the liquid into his mouth.

Feeling a strange sense of bonding with the baby, Rose rocked him until he went to sleep. Holding him on her shoulder, she entered the bedroom. Moody again knelt beside the bed, holding his wife's hand. By the dim light of the oil lamp, Rose saw the naked pain in the man's eyes. He remained there until almost daylight, when with a weary sigh, Martha Moody breathed her last.

"She's gone, Mr. Moody," Lottie said quietly.

He buried his head on his wife's breast, and his body shook with sobs. When he stood, he handed Lottie a bag of coins. "Will you take care of her burial? This is enough to pay for your services and the cost of burying her. I cannot delay any longer. The boat's captain said he would lay over for the night in Louisville. I'll be leaving when he does."

Wearily, he moved toward the door. Rose stepped forward and thrust the baby toward him. "Don't forget your son."

He stared at her with blank eyes. Without even looking at the face of his child, he said, "I don't want him—you keep him."

one

The weather was typical of an April morning in Kentucky. The greening grass glistened in the morning dew. Cardinals sang cheerfully from the tops of the evergreen trees. Rose Thurston pulled the reins of the sorrel mare and guided her Brewster phaeton into Cave Hill Cemetery. Following the irregular terrain past the gravestones of early Louisville settlers, she stopped the vehicle in a section of more recent graves.

Martin, her sandy-haired son, picked up a bouquet of flowers, jumped out of the carriage, and hurried through the dewy grass, scattering a pair of nesting doves as he ran.

Martin Moody Thurston had been born ten years ago today. As Rose followed him she wondered what Edward Moody would think if he could see his son now. After Moody's rapid departure, Rose and Lottie had used all of their limited medical expertise to keep the child alive. After it was certain that the boy would live, Lottie gave most of the child's care into Rose's hands. When she turned twenty-one, Rose had legally adopted the boy.

Through the years, Rose had expected Edward Moody to return for his son, but she had heard nothing from him since the day he had rushed from their shanty boat. Although Martin was small for his age, he was an intelligent, good-hearted boy, who had been a blessing to Rose and her grandparents. Always in the back of Rose's mind was the concern that his father might return to take Martin away from her.

"Look, Mama," Martin called, as he laid his flowers at the base of a five-foot, recently installed, marble angel. "Isn't this pretty? Wouldn't my mother be proud of it?"

The base of the monument bore the epitaph—

MARTHA, WIFE OF EDWARD MOODY
DIED APRIL 5, 1876.

Rose had kept the memory of his mother alive for Martin by bringing him to the cemetery several times a year, and always on his birthday, also the date of his mother's death.

Lottie and Harry had used some of the gold coins Edward Moody had left for Martha Moody's burial, but the small headstone they had erected had deteriorated through the years. The Thurstons had invested the rest of his father's money for Martin, when he came of age, so Rose had replaced the stone at her own expense.

"I'll clip some of the grass from the lot," Rose said, "while you bring the food basket from the carriage." It wasn't often that the weather was pleasant enough for a picnic on Martin's birthday, so this added to their joy of the day.

Martin gave Rose an impulsive hug. "Thank you, Mama, for bringing me here. I love you, but I also love my first mother."

Rose ruffled his crisp, straw-colored hair, which was like his father's. Often during the night his wife died, Rose had watched Edward Moody thread his trembling fingers through his crisp hair. Rose had noticed the same characteristic in her son, marveling that Martin exhibited so many traits of this father he had never seen. She had wondered often about Edward, praying that he had found peace from the loss of his family. As she had watched Martin grow, she was saddened that his father had missed all of those important years.

When Martin returned with the food, Rose said, "I'm about finished. Take the basket over to that big rock. The ground is too wet here."

When she reached the picnic site, Martin had already spread a blanket over the rock outcropping beside a towering cedar tree. Opening the picnic basket, Rose said, "Let's see what Sallie fixed for our picnic."

She lifted out a small plate of fried chicken and handed it to Martin.

"Oh, boy," he said, passing the plate back and forth under his nose, sniffing appreciatively.

Rose unwrapped several slices of wheat bread and put two apples on the blanket between them.

"Let's say a prayer of thanks before we start to eat." She took Martin's hand. "God, we're thankful for such a beautiful day after the storms of this week. I pray for the protection of those who are threatened by flooding. I thank You for Martin and the blessing he's been to me. Help him to have a good birthday. We're grateful also for the food. We pray for protection through this day. We love You. Amen."

"Is this all the food Sallie sent?" Martin asked.

Arching her eyebrows, Rose said, "Well, what else could you want? We've got chicken, fresh bread, and apples."

"I thought she might have put in something sweet."

Reaching inside the basket again, she pulled out a plate of chocolate cake. "Oh, you mean like this."

Martin clapped his hands. "Sallie knows that's my favorite."

After they finished eating, Rose and Martin walked toward the section of the cemetery where Civil War soldiers, both Union and Confederate, were buried. Martin always liked to come here, not only to wander among the headstones but also to play in the pond at the base of the hill. Their walk was shortened when the sun disappeared behind a cloud and a few raindrops fell.

"I think we'd better start for home," Rose said. "I had hoped that the rain was over. If the river rises another foot, a lot of houses will be flooded."

The rain was still light when they reached the covered phaeton, and Rose drove slowly through the narrow lanes of the cemetery. At one spot, she had a slight view of the

Ohio River. A week of rain had swollen the river, and many steamboats were tied up in the harbor, waiting until the floodwaters passed. Wharf buildings closest to the river were submerged in the muddy water, and the boats were on a level with the tops of some of the structures.

Martin stood up. "I see the *Vagabond*."

Her grandfather's shanty boat was easily recognized, for Lottie Thurston had painted the name in large red letters across the front of the boat. Rose would have recognized it without the name, for the *Vagabond* had been home to her for most of her life. She knew every nook and cranny of the boat by memory.

"Gramps is probably sitting on the deck catching some fresh catfish for your birthday dinner tonight. He knows how to catch fish in spite of the muddy water."

Grinning, Martin answered, "And I bet Granny is baking a birthday cake for me."

Rose ruffled his thick hair. "She's always trying to put some weight on you."

Martin looked at his bony arms with distaste. "You say my father was a big man."

"Tall, with massive shoulders and strong, sturdy legs. His head almost grazed the ceiling of the *Vagabond*, and the boat shook under his weight when he walked."

A sad expression darkened Martin's eyes, and he said, "Wonder why he didn't want me?"

As she had done numerous times before, Rose tried to justify Edward Moody's actions in giving his child away.

"I've told you how weak and sickly you were. It took Granny and me months to make you well. You would have died if he had taken you with him."

"But why couldn't he wait until I got better?"

"I don't know," Rose said patiently, as if she hadn't answered this question many times.

"And why hasn't he come back for me?"

"I don't know that, either."

"Maybe he died like my mother."

"That's a possibility."

"I know one thing," Martin said, with a stubborn facial expression also reminiscent of his father. "If he ever does come back, I won't have anything to do with him."

"Now if that isn't a gloomy face for a birthday boy to have!" Rose chided him.

A roll of thunder threatened another shower, so Rose lifted the reins and urged the horse toward home.

Rose still couldn't believe she was actually living in an Italian Renaissance Revival home, where she felt like a fish out of water. A shanty boat girl living in a palatial mansion in the heart of downtown Louisville! But when John Boardman, a man whose life she had saved, had died a year ago and left his fortune to her, for Martin's sake she had moved into the Boardman house. She still didn't like going to bed without feeling the flow of the Ohio River beneath her, but surely in time she would get used to being a rich woman.

Boardman had built his home on a two-acre plot. The house fronted on Third Street, but he had provided for servants' quarters, a stable, and a carriage shed in the backyard. In deference to his neighbors, he had camouflaged the utility structures with a hedge of evergreens. Rose drove the phaeton into the carriage house, and Sallie's husband, Isaiah Taylor, came running to help her unhitch the mare.

The Taylors had worked for John Boardman for several years, and Rose more or less inherited them along with the house. She didn't know how she could have handled the change in her social status without them. She considered Sallie and Isaiah among her best friends.

"I feared you wouldn't make it home before the storm," Isaiah said. "I sure figgered you'd get wet, Miss Rose."

She telegraphed a message to Isaiah with her eyes, and he nodded, a big smile spreading across his face. He unhitched the mare from the phaeton.

"Before we go into the house, Martin, you might want to take a look at your birthday present."

"Where is it?" Martin asked.

"Isaiah will show you."

"Right this way, sonny," Isaiah said, leading the mare toward the stalls in the adjoining stable. Martin trotted beside him, and Rose followed. After he put the mare in her stall, Isaiah pointed to an adjoining enclosure.

"Happy birthday!" Isaiah and Rose shouted in unison.

"A pony," Martin whispered in awe.

"You made a good choice, Isaiah," Rose said as she looked at the black pony that moved docilely toward them.

Isaiah gave Martin an ear of corn, and he held it out to the pony. "Here, Tibbets." As the pony nibbled on the corn, Martin turned to Rose. "I've always thought if I ever had a pony, I'd call him Tibbets."

"But why?" Rose asked, laughing. "Where did you ever hear that name?"

He shrugged his shoulders. "It came to me in a dream one time." He hurried to Rose and threw his arms around her waist. "Thank you, Mama."

She knelt and returned his embrace. "Thank you for being my boy," she said. Burying her face in his curls, tears formed in Rose's eyes.

"When can I ride him?"

Rose looked to Isaiah for an answer. Thunder rolled across the roof of the barn, and a lightning bolt flashed over their heads. "Not until this storm is over," he said.

"Remember, Martin," Rose cautioned. "No riding for a few weeks unless Isaiah or I are with you. You understand?"

"Yes, ma'am."

❧

The rain had stopped by the time Rose and Martin started toward the river. Although it was several blocks, Rose preferred to walk. As the river had risen, Harry Thurston had shortened the lines on the *Vagabond*, and when he saw them coming, he lowered a wide board to the bank for them to cross. Rose had no fear of the water, nor did Martin, for the river had been his home for most of his life, too. They walked across the small, bouncy bridge without a glance toward the water.

"Hi, Gramps. Did you know about my pony?"

"A pony for your birthday! How about that? A big house to live in and now a pony. You're gonna get too proud for your old grandpa."

"No!" Martin shouted. Running to Harry, he hugged him so tightly that Harry staggered, and Rose moved quickly to steady her grandfather. His legs were crippled with rheumatism, and Harry had lost the youthful vigor that Rose had always admired.

"Careful," Rose cautioned Martin, as she held her grandfather's arm until he steadied himself.

"I didn't mean to hurt you, Grandpa. But I'll never be too rich for you. Why don't you come and live with Mama and me?"

"No, son," Harry said. "I was born in a boat on this river, and I aim to die here."

"What's all this commotion I hear?" Lottie said, appearing behind them in the kitchen door.

"Hi, Granny," Rose said. "Need any help?"

"Nary a bit. Everything's about ready."

"Have you heard any predictions about the water crest?" Rose asked.

"Nothing official," Harry said. "But the rise is less than an inch an hour, so I figure it's tapering off."

"At least this late in the season," Lottie said; "we won't have to worry about the river freezing and the boats breaking apart when the river goes down."

When she had lived with her grandparents, Rose had taken the rise and fall of the river for granted. But now she worried about her grandparents living alone. And she was also concerned about the showboat she had inherited from John Boardman.

She should have known that Harry would sense her concern, for as they moved into the room that served as a joint kitchen and living area, he said, "I checked out the *Silver Queen* today."

"Everything all right?"

"Yep. I went aboard and had a look-see. Best I can tell, the two watchmen have everything under control. They were asking if you're still intendin' to take the showboat out by the first of June."

"Yes, I am, Lord willing. And I hope they will stay with the boat for another two months. Martin will be out of school by then." As they gathered around the small table, she added, "I'm scared to even consider it, but I owe it to Mr. Boardman to carry on the tradition of the *Silver Queen*."

They gathered around the table that was nailed to the floor to keep it steady when the river was rough. Lottie not only had fried catfish, but she had boiled greens picked from a nearby field, mashed potatoes, hominy, baked corn pone, and a two-layer spice cake.

After supper, Harry moved to his rocking chair and said, " 'Pears like I'm the only one who ain't given the birthday boy a present. Lottie fixed the good supper. Rose bought a pony. What do you want from me, sonny?"

"Give me the leather bag my father left behind with money in it," Martin said without hesitation. Rose's shoulders slumped, and she dropped her head. Regardless of what she did, she couldn't rid Martin of the desire to know more about his past. Poor child! The only physical connections to his parents were the grave in Cave Hill Cemetery and the leather bag that his father had once held.

Harry shrugged his shoulders and, with a resigned expression on his face, went to a cupboard in their bedroom. From the top shelf he took down a leather bag.

"All right, Martin—you've asked for it enough times, and

today it's yours. But," he added when Martin reached for the bag, "you must leave it here in the shanty until you're a man."

Martin nodded, took the bag, and sat on the floor. Silently, he ran his fingers over the bag and turned it inside out, as if searching for a clue to his parentage. He looked long at the document of deposit in one of Louisville's banks. After Martha Moody's burial expenses had been paid, there were still over a hundred dollars in gold coins left. The money had been deposited in Martin's name, with Harry as trustee, so he would have a little nest egg when he became of age. In light of Rose's inheritance from John Boardman, she would have enough for Martin's education, but noting the expression on his face, she thanked God that Martin had something tangible to remind him of his father.

Rose turned to take the dishes off the table, when a sudden surge of water caused the shanty to list sideways. Two plates toppled to the floor and shattered into small pieces—the sound as startling as a gunshot. Behind her, Lottie lost her balance and fell to her knees.

"What's going on?" Harry said, as he struggled out of the rocking chair and headed for the door. Something struck the *Vagabond* with a deadening impact. Harry's rocking chair slid across the floor and collided with the kitchen table, barely missing Martin, who still sat on the floor.

Rose helped her grandmother into a chair. "Hold on, Gramps," she said. "I'll see what's happened." She had just reached the door, when the shanty boat lurched again. "Gramps!" she shouted. "We're moving!"

Holding to the wall, Harry moved out on the deck, with Rose behind him. The terror on her grandfather's face stunned Rose.

A barge loaded with coal was moving down the river just a few yards beyond them. "That barge must have broken loose from its moorings," she said. "That's what hit us."

"And hit hard enough to snap our ropes, too."

"What can we do, Gramps?"

"There ain't nothin' we can do except pray. I beached our skiff until the water went down."

Now that the water had almost reached flood level, the Ohio was as smooth as a lake, and there was no danger of the shanty capsizing in turbulent waves. But what could they do? The *Vagabond* was not self-propelled. If the boat would stay close to the bank, it might be possible to catch hold of tree limbs and pull it toward the bank or into a small creek inlet. But it was heading toward the main channel of the Ohio.

Lottie peered out of the kitchen door, with Martin hanging on to her apron. "One blessing is that there's not many boats on the river right now," she said calmly.

During the past sixty years, Lottie had survived many crises on the river, and her calmness encouraged Rose. Her grandmother scanned the western horizon where the sun was setting in a red sky with a few black clouds. "We've got about an hour of daylight left."

Harry dropped to his knees on the deck. "Lord, You saved the disciples when things got out of control on the Sea of Galilee. I believe You have as much control over the Ohio River as You did that little lake. The scripture tells us that 'the Lord is nigh unto all them that call upon him.' Well, Lord, I'm callin' on You now. Send help so's my family won't perish. Don't matter about me and Lottie—we've been yearnin' to go home for a good many years. But Martin and Rose has got their whole lives before them. Save them by Your mercy, O Lord. Amen."

Catching hold of a railing, Harry struggled to his feet.

"I believe in the power of prayer," he said to Rose, who moved cautiously to his side and sat down beside him on a bench.

"Mama," Martin cried from the doorway. "I'm afraid."

Rose motioned to him, and he rushed to her side. She hugged him close. "I'm a little afraid, too, but Gramps prayed.

God is in control of our lives. We'll be all right."

They traveled past Goose Island and Rock Island and swung into a large curve, which cut off their view of the city of Louisville. Normally, Rose would have enjoyed the voyage because she was never happier than when she was floating on the river, but her pulse beat erratically, and a tight knot formed in her stomach. Several people on the bank waved to them, and Rose wondered if these people thought they were on a pleasure trip.

"There's a ferry landing down the river a ways," Harry said. "If the owner is on his ferry flat, he might be able to come out and snag the *Vagabond*."

"But will we reach there before dark?" Rose asked, with a worried glance at the darkening western sky.

Harry shook his head. After they passed the mouth of a large creek, the water was swifter, and the *Vagabond* picked up speed. The frail craft listed to the left when they rounded a bend in the river faster than Rose thought was safe. But in the twilight, she saw a bulky shape ahead of them.

"Look, Gramps! There's a towboat tied up to the left. Granny, bring some pillowcases. If we wave them, the passengers on that boat will know there's somebody aboard. Get some pots, Martin, and start pounding on them."

Harry stood and peered intently forward. "That's the *Mary Ann*, and she's got steam up. Cap Parsons will be on board."

In spite of his twisted limbs, Harry danced a little jig around the deck. When he saw the small stern-wheeler edge away from the bank, he shouted, "They've seen us! Hallelujah! Praise the Lord! 'Bless the Lord, O my soul; and all that is within me, bless His holy name.'"

Rose recognized their friend, Captain Parsons, in the pilothouse. The larger steamboats usually had both a captain and a pilot, but Parsons had his pilot's license, and he steered his boat most of the time.

Half a dozen or more men lined the lower deck of the

steamboat. Two of them were coiling ropes. One large man stood out from the rest, not only because of his size, but because he was dressed in a suit and tie. He appeared to be a passenger rather than a deckhand. Two other men leaned outward, holding long hooks on heavy chains.

When the towboat came closer, Captain Parsons, a tall, lanky river man, guffawed gleefully. "Hey there, Harry!" he shouted, and the sound echoed across the water. "How did an old river rat like you get set adrift on the Ohio?"

"It ain't funny, Cap, and none of my doing, either. Quit your jawin' and hook on to this boat. I don't want to lose my home."

When the towboat was within ten feet of the *Vagabond*, the men dropped ropes around the posts at each end of the shanty. The two hooks were thrown to the fore and aft decks and snagged the wooden floor. The boat came to a sudden halt, and Rose heard more dishes sliding off the kitchen table. But what did that matter? As long as they were safe, she could replace her grandmother's dishes.

The *Mary Ann* backed slowly toward the shore, pulling the shanty boat behind it. Rose had never felt such relief, such thankfulness to God, than she did when the captain of the towboat swung the *Vagabond* toward the bank. Two of the crewmen jumped to the deck of the shanty boat and helped Harry secure their home to the towboat as well as to a large tree along the bank.

Calling from the deck of his boat, Captain Parsons invited, "Come over here so we can talk. I want to find out what happened to you. Any damage to the *Vagabond*?"

Lottie came out of the shanty where she'd gone to inspect it. "Just a few broken dishes," she told Captain Parsons. "We were blessed."

Martin volunteered to help his grandmother set the furniture right in the shanty. Rose followed her grandfather to the deck of the bigger boat. The large, well-dressed man she had noted earlier reached out a hand to help her. She didn't need any help, but she didn't want to be impolite. She placed her hand in his and reached the deck of the packet boat safely. She looked up to thank him and staggered backward. Although ten years had made many changes, Rose knew she wasn't mistaken. Edward Moody had returned at last!

two

Rose looked wildly about to be sure Martin hadn't followed her. Harry and Captain Parsons were in a deep discussion of the shanty's chances of survival in such an accident.

Edward Moody removed his hat and took her by the arm. "Ma'am, are you ill? Come and sit down."

He directed her toward a bench that was out of sight of the others, and Rose went gladly, for she didn't know if her legs would hold her erect much longer. Apparently Edward Moody had no idea who she was. In her fashionable clothing, she didn't much resemble the eighteen-year-old who, ten years ago, had been dressed in an ankle-length gingham dress without any bustle or extra petticoats. And, of course, he hadn't paid any attention to her—he had eyes only for his wife. He had no time for Rose or his son.

Rose had often wondered what she would do if she ever saw Edward Moody again. Would she treat him charitably? Would she bawl him out for deserting his son? If he didn't recognize his child, would she tell him who Martin was? Why had he returned to Kentucky? Her mind rioted with questions that had no answer while she prayed for the wisdom to deal with Martin's father.

When he had her settled comfortably, Edward said, "That was a narrow escape. It's little wonder that you are upset. How did you happen to be on the boat?"

"The shanty was tied up at Louisville, and I was on the boat visiting my grandparents. A barge broke loose from its moorings and careened into the *Vagabond*. Gramps had put his skiff on higher ground to get it out of the floodwaters. We didn't have any way to escape." She decided to drop a hint to see if he recalled their previous meeting. "I'm Rose Thurston."

His facial expression didn't change. She couldn't believe that her name and the shanty boat wouldn't tantalize his memory.

"My name is Edward Moody. I bought passage on the *Mary Ann* at Cairo. I have some business in Louisville."

Having a pretty good idea of what his business in Louisville was, Rose's pulse quickened, and anxious thoughts scurried around in her mind. Had he come looking for his son? Or perhaps to find the grave of his wife? Did he remember that this was the anniversary of his wife's death? Would it be possible for her to hide Martin from him?

"Come and get your vittles," a loud command came from the *Mary Ann*'s galley.

Rose stood and thanked Edward for his help. Captain Parsons joined them. "Rose, do you want to eat supper with us?"

"No, thanks. We had just finished our evening meal when the accident happened. I'm going back to the shanty to see if Granny needs any help."

"The water is falling now, and I'm aiming to head upriver in the morning. I told Harry I'd tow him back to his landing."

"Thanks, Captain. It won't be the first time you've towed the *Vagabond* from one port to the other. You've been a good friend to the Thurstons."

Edward reached for Rose's hand, and she placed hers in it. "I enjoyed our brief meeting, Miss Thurston," he said. "I'm a stranger to Louisville. Since I intend to stop over for a few days, I'd like to see you again. Will you give me your address and permission to contact you?"

Rose hesitated momentarily. "I live in the Boardman house on Third Street. Most anyone can tell you where it is."

"Perhaps we can have dinner together some evening."

"Thank you. I would like that."

Rose wasn't sure she would like it, but she intended to keep aware of Edward Moody's activities in Louisville.

Apparently during the excitement of being rescued, none of her family had noticed Rose talking to the stranger, for no questions were asked. Rose helped Lottie clean up the few broken dishes, and they returned the furnishings to their normal positions.

Harry had never learned to read, but he sat in his rocker, holding the Bible until Rose and Lottie finished the work. It was a nightly ritual to read a chapter from the Bible and have prayer before going to bed.

Martin sat on the floor at Harry's feet, and Rose and Lottie drew their chairs close. Harry handed the Bible to Rose. "I've been ponderin' about the many times in the Bible when God delivered His people. And I'm hankerin' to have you read about the time God saved the apostle Paul and his friends during a shipwreck."

"That story is in the last part of the book of Acts, Gramps." Glancing at Martin, whose eyes were already drooping sleepily, Rose added, "I won't read the whole chapter."

"You won't have to," Lottie said. "During our years on the river, I've read them chapters often. We know the apostle Paul was on a boat that even the captain thought would be lost, until Paul received the revelation that God would save them."

"Read the part about the angel coming to speak to Paul, Mama," Martin said.

Putting his hand on Martin's head, Harry said, "That's the part I want to hear, too, sonny. I didn't hear no angel talkin' to me when we were tumblin' down the river, but God must have had a whole legion of angels keepin' the *Vagabond* afloat tonight."

"I'll start where Paul related God's message to his shipmates," Rose said. " 'And now I exhort you to be of good cheer: for there shall be no loss of any man's life among you, but of the ship. For there stood by me this night the angel of God, whose I am, and whom I serve, saying, Fear not, Paul; thou must be brought before Caesar: and lo, God hath given thee all them that sail with thee. Wherefore, sirs, be of good cheer:

for I believe God, that it shall be even as it was told me.'"

Easing his body out of the rocker, Harry knelt by his chair. "Lord God, we come to You humbly tonight, knowing that we ain't done nothin' to deserve Your goodness. We also know, God, that even if we had gone down with the *Vagabond*, that wouldn't mean Your hand was agin' us. As long as we've got promise of a home in heaven, nothin' can separate us from Your love. Paul the apostle was a great man, Lord, and I call to mind his words in the book of Romans when he said that nothin' would be able to separate us from the love of God, which is in Christ Jesus our Lord. Amen."

Rose wiped her eyes when her grandfather finished praying. Although he had not had an opportunity to be educated, from listening to Lottie and Rose read the scripture, Harry had a vast knowledge of God's Word. Conscious of their lack of education, he and Lottie had sacrificed to send Rose to a girls' academy. How much she owed these two people who'd taken her in when her parents had died!

Martin and Harry settled for the night in her grandparents' bed, while Lottie put sheets and quilts on the bed Rose had occupied before she had moved into the Boardman house. Rose extinguished all lights except one lamp chained to the kitchen table before she joined her grandmother. Lottie was already in bed. Rose left the door slightly ajar to provide enough light to feel her way around the room to remove her clothes and put on one of Lottie's voluminous nightgowns. She sat on the edge of the bed.

"What's troubling you, honey?" Lottie asked quietly.

"Did you see the man I was talking to on the *Mary Ann*?"

"Not close-up. I didn't heed him in particular."

"It was Edward Moody."

Lottie sat upright in bed, and the springs squeaked and bounced under her weight. "Are you sure?"

"I recognized him at once, but he introduced himself."

"Did he know who you were?"

Rose shook her head; then realizing that Lottie couldn't see in the semidarkness, she said, "No. I gave him several hints, but apparently the events of ten years ago didn't stay in his mind. I'm afraid of him, Granny."

"Wasn't he from Pittsburgh? Maybe he'll head on upriver and not stop at Louisville."

"No. He's going to stay for a while. He told me he had some business in Louisville. I know what that business will be."

Rubbing Rose's back with her chubby hand, Lottie asked, "You didn't tell him about the boy?"

"I hadn't decided what to do when the cook announced supper, and that gave me a short reprieve to think about it."

"Now that the water is falling, the steamboats will be movin' out. Harry can find a boat to pull us downriver, and we could stay until Moody leaves."

"I've thought of that, but I shouldn't take Martin out of school. Because he was such a puny baby, Mr. Moody probably thinks the child died, and he might just be looking for his wife's grave. But if he starts asking questions, he'll soon learn about Martin. Besides, I wouldn't feel right not to tell Martin that his father has returned."

"I know. Poor little tyke, all these years he's still so hurt because his father gave him away," Lottie answered, settling down on the mattress.

"Mr. Moody invited me to have dinner with him some evening, and I intend to accept. Perhaps I can find out what he means to do."

Rose lay down beside her grandmother and pulled one of Lottie's quilts over her shoulders. "I hope I can keep Martin and his father separated until we get back to Louisville. I need a little time to prepare for it."

"I'll tell Harry to keep Martin occupied and not let him go over on the *Mary Ann*."

"Yes, do that," Rose agreed, turning over and finally falling into a fretful sleep.

Since life on the river was commonplace to Martin, Harry didn't have any trouble keeping the child busy. He had always enjoyed playing with the Shawnee arrowheads that Harry had collected through the years. When he tired of that, while the *Mary Ann* pushed their home steadily upriver, Lottie asked him to help her cut out quilt blocks.

Harry owned a narrow strip of land a short distance south of the Louisville landing, and the shanty boat was pushed safely into place. Rose stayed out of sight until the *Mary Ann* docked farther upstream. By early afternoon, without seeing any more of Edward Moody, Rose prepared to start home.

A worried look on her face, Lottie said quietly to Rose as they were leaving, "I'll be praying for God's will to be done in this matter."

Rose hugged her grandmother. "And please pray for me to have the grace to accept His will."

"God understands, honey. Remember, He gave up *His* son!"

"I remembered that all night long. I want what is best for Martin. I'm grateful for the few hours I've had to come to terms with this before I have to confront Mr. Moody."

"Don't forget that Martin is old enough to have a say in the matter, too."

"Come on, Mama," Martin called from the bank. "I want to get home to my pony."

Waving good-bye to her grandparents, Rose crossed the gangplank and started toward their house. She took the less-traveled streets because she wasn't yet ready to encounter Edward Moody.

Since Rose and Martin had not yet been home following the near tragedy, Sallie and Isaiah hadn't heard about the Thurstons' narrow escape.

"Praise God," Isaiah said when Rose told him what had happened. "The Lord sure had His hand on you."

While Martin excitedly explained their runaway experience

to Isaiah, Rose drew Sallie to one side and quietly told her about the return of Martin's father.

"I don't want Martin to know until I find out what Mr. Moody's intentions are. But is that right? He's anticipated his father's return for years. Should I tell him?"

"Use your own best judgment, Miss Rose. But if you want my advice, I can't see that it will hurt to keep the truth from him a day or two."

"That's what Granny thought, too," Rose said. "Mr. Moody indicated that he might invite me to dinner. If he doesn't do that soon, I'll make it a point to see him."

"The boy is excited about his pony now. That'll keep his mind busy for several days."

"Tell Isaiah that I may want him to keep an eye on Mr. Moody."

❧

After getting directions from Captain Parsons for a suitable hotel, Edward left the waterfront and walked up the bank. The falling water had left several inches of mud on the streets, and his boots were crusted with brown silt when he reached the Galt House recommended to him by Captain Parsons. Although water had surrounded the hotel, the interior had not been flooded. Workers were busily cleaning mud from the Main Street entrance.

When he registered, the clerk asked Edward how many days he expected to stay.

"I'm not sure," he said. "Possibly a week or more."

After learning the times meals were served and asking for bath water to be delivered to his room, Edward walked up the carpeted circular stairway to the second floor. It had been a long, arduous journey from Colorado to Kentucky.

Was he following a dream? Or would he have been wiser to have stayed in Colorado? He had set out ten years ago to make his fortune. He had accomplished that dream, but he had soon found out that wealth did not bring happiness. Six months ago he had broken his leg, and while he was immobile for several weeks, he had come to terms with his mistakes of the past. The loss of his family gnawed constantly at his peace of mind. And his relationship with God had suffered during the years when he slaved to achieve his goal.

For long periods of time, Edward had successfully pushed thoughts of the past into the background. But those times when he couldn't forget, his heart became burdened with guilt because he had left his wife for others to bury.

He had never forgotten the girl on the shanty boat who had accused him of killing his wife by taking her on a long journey when she was with child. The fear that the girl may have been right had caused him hundreds of sleepless nights. He had loved Martha wholeheartedly, and no other woman had been able to take her place in his heart. Regardless of why she had died, he should have stayed long enough to see that she received a decent burial. He had left plenty of money for the woman to see to her burial, but he couldn't forget that it was his responsibility.

When he got to that point, he always justified his actions by reminding himself that if he hadn't arrived in Colorado by the first of May, he would have lost the opportunity to invest in the gold mine. Then he would be disgusted at himself for being so persistent. God had thrown all kinds of roadblocks in his way to keep him from putting his money in an investment that was doomed to failure from the first. But, oh no, he wouldn't listen to God or pay any attention to His signs. Edward Moody always knew best!

And what about their baby? Surely the child had died just as his mother had, but he should have stayed until he knew for sure. Had he been disloyal to Martha by not looking after the child she'd given him at the expense of her own life? Was it too late to make restitution?

If the child still lived, he intended to rescue him from the life of poverty he must have endured because he was an orphan. How could he find out if his child still lived?

In desperation, Edward bowed his head on the small table in his room. *God, I haven't been a faithful believer. I've been too busy following my own star to take time to give You any part of my life. God, I'm not asking for myself now. But if the boy lives, will You help me find him so I can make up for the years he's had to live in poverty?*

It had been days since he had slept in a bed, and Edward needed to rest. He decided to postpone his investigation until the next day. Perhaps by that time, in His graciousness, God would give him an answer. Sleep didn't come easily to him, and he thought of Rose Thurston. Perhaps if he arranged to see her she could help him solve the mystery of what had happened to his wife and child.

❧

After a fitful night's sleep, Edward was still without divine direction. He ate a hearty breakfast in the dining room, thinking of yesterday's experiences. With the memory of his wife always in the back of his mind, Edward hadn't been interested in women. In spite of the temptations put in his way in the towns spawned by Colorado's booming mining industry, he had lived a celibate life. So why was his mind preoccupied with the woman he had met the day before? How was she different from other women he had ignored? Perhaps it was her appearance. Her sparkling dark blue eyes reminded him of the ocean's waves. Her bronze-gold hair braided and wrapped around her head looked like a golden crown. Several times he caught himself wondering what her hair would look like hanging loose over her shoulders.

Was it too soon to ask her to have dinner with him? She hadn't discouraged him when he mentioned the possibility. He stopped by the desk when he finished his meal.

"Do you have a messenger service?" he queried the clerk.

"Yes, sir," the man said. He pointed to a desk at one side of the lobby. "You will find paper and pen on that table. You write your message, and we will deliver it any place in the city, free of charge."

Edward sat at the table, nervously trying to decide what to say. Grimly, he thought he was as indecisive as a boy. After all, he only wanted to have dinner with the woman. He wasn't asking her to marry him. Deciding that brevity was the best approach, he finally penned:

> *Miss Thurston,*
>   *I would like to further our acquaintance. I've checked out the restaurant at the Galt House and find it adequate. If you're available to have dinner with me tonight, name a time convenient for you and give me directions to your home, so I can call for you. I will await your answer through the messenger.*
>
> *Edward Moody*

Edward read the message and frowned. He certainly hadn't been brief, and the message sounded stilted. Perhaps he should give her more time and suggest a later date, but his mission was urgent. He didn't know how long he would be in Louisville, but he knew he wanted to see Rose Thurston again before he left the city.

He hadn't had much experience inviting ladies to dinner. Not knowing any better way to compose the invitation, he blotted the note, sealed it, and backed the envelope with the address Rose had mentioned. He took the letter to the desk clerk.

"Please have the return message brought to my room," he said, as he pressed a gold coin into the man's hand.

❧

Rose was at the paddock watching Martin ride the pony when the messenger found her. She read the message and called Isaiah to stay with Martin while she returned to the house. She had known the messenger boy for years, so she invited him to come into the kitchen with her.

"Sallie, give Russell a piece of cake and some milk while I write a response to this message. Then come to the office for a few minutes, please." She was still poring over the letter five minutes later when Sallie entered the office. Rose read the message to her.

"What should I do? I more or less agreed to have a meal with him, but should I put him off for a day or two?"

"You'll fret about it until you do go, won't you?" Sallie queried, grinning widely.

"You know me too well, Sallie. Yes, I suppose I will."

"Then you might as well go and get it over with."

"That's the way I feel about it. I'll go this evening. But I don't want him to come to this house and see Martin. Will you ask Isaiah if he can drive me to the hotel at six thirty? I'd drive myself, but," she added with a wry grin, "I suppose that isn't the way a lady should conduct herself."

Laughing, Sallie said, "Oh, you're doing better, Miss Rose. I'll go and feed Russell some more cake while you pen the note."

After Russell had been sent on his way, Rose turned again to Sallie for advice. Sallie had worked for society matrons off and on for years, so she was a good mentor for Rose.

"So what am I going to wear, and how am I going to keep Martin from knowing what I'm doing?"

"Wear that new gown you bought last week from Miss Spencer's boutique. And don't fret about Martin—I'll watch out for him. He thinks it's fun to eat in the kitchen with Isaiah and me. And after supper, Isaiah can teach him to curry his pony."

The rest of the afternoon dragged for Rose. She couldn't settle down to do anything. She walked from one room to the other until she was aggravated with herself. Finally she called to Sallie. "I'm going to walk down to the *Vagabond*. Watch Martin, please."

"Sure enough! But don't stay too long. It may take some time to get dressed."

Rose threw a woolen shawl over her shoulders, for a strong wind blew from the river. Signs of spring were around her, however. A mockingbird, perched on a white picket fence, ran through his entire repertoire of birdcalls. Patches of violets lent a purple hue to many of the yards along Third Street. A cardinal's insistent *cheer, cheer* echoed like a trumpet over her head. By the time she reached the waterfront, Rose's temperament was back to normal.

She found Lottie alone on the shanty, patching one of Harry's shirts.

"I may have made a mistake, Granny," Rose said, sitting on the floor beside her grandmother.

"So," Lottie said, "everybody's got a right to make a mistake now and again."

Calmed even more by Lottie's complacent attitude, Rose told her about Edward's invitation and her acceptance. "Should I have refused? Would it have been better to put him off for a few days?"

Lottie laid the shirt aside and, with a work-roughened hand, smoothed Rose's hair back from her forehead. "Always thinking of others before your own self. You're trying to protect Martin. But do you actually think you can keep Moody from learning about his son? People like to think of Louisville as a city, and I reckon it is, but it's still a small town at heart where anybody's business is common knowledge. All the man has to do is ask a few questions, and he will soon learn that Martin is his boy."

"And Martin will have to be told. I'm not sure if I should come right out and tell Mr. Moody or let him find out on his own. This dinner should give me an opportunity to find out what he's really like before I introduce him to Martin."

"I agree. It won't hurt to let one more day pass before you tell the boy."

Feeling better, Rose hurried back home.

ₑ

Since there was still some coolness in the spring night air, Rose decided that she would be comfortable in the new dress she had bought the week before. Sallie arranged most of Rose's hair on top of her head, with curly bangs and a long fall of hair to her shoulders. She tied the corset strings and arranged the petticoats and bustle before Rose put on the two-piece dress.

Miss Spencer had told Rose that the garment was really a house dress, but considering the everyday dresses she had worn most of her life, the garment seemed elegant to her. The dress was styled from printed silk and plain satin in shades of blue. The long-sleeved bodice had a lawn collar and cuffs, and it extended over her slender hips. The tie-back skirt, trimmed with pleating and large bows, was floor-length with a modest ruffled train.

Although she felt as if she were bound in fetters, looking in the mirror, she knew that she was in the stylish mode of the day and probably wearing the kind of clothing Edward Moody expected of a woman.

As the crowning touch, Sallie set a velvet hat with ruched silk under the brim, trimmed with a curled ostrich feather on her head. Rose made a face at her image in the mirror.

Sallie chuckled. "Now, Miss Rose, you're beautiful and you know it."

"Beauty shouldn't be skin deep. In deciding whether I'm a fit mother for his son, Mr. Moody should look beyond all of this finery."

Sallie gave Rose a quick hug. "Don't worry. He'll see the real you. You couldn't change your true nature if you tried."

Despite her affluence, Rose hadn't aspired to become a part of Louisville's social life, but she did want Martin to be accepted when he was older. Conscious of this fact, she always exerted an effort to act like a lady-born when she was in public. Fortunately, she had learned how to be ladylike when she attended Miss Bordeaux's academy.

❧

Edward waited for her in the lobby, and when he saw Isaiah help her from the carriage, he hurried down the steps to the street. She extended her hand, and when Edward touched it briefly with his lips, she wasn't prepared for her reaction to his touch.

Dear God, help me to remember that I'm here on Martin's behalf.

Touching her elbow, Edward directed her toward the dining room. Gaslights were available in the city now, but the Galt House dining room still had enormous crystal chandeliers lit by candles. Edward and Rose were ushered to a secluded alcove, also lit by candles. They ordered the specialty of the day—roast beef, baked potatoes, green beans, and freshly baked bread.

After the waiter left, wanting to find out all she could about Edward, Rose said, "Do you expect to spend a long time in Louisville?"

"I'm not sure. I'm rather footloose at the present. I used to live in Pittsburgh, but I've been in Colorado since 1876. I arrived there a few months before it entered the Union. I suppose you could say I grew up with the state."

"Then you intend to return to Colorado?"

He shrugged his shoulders. "I don't know. I had expected to make Colorado my home, but my plans didn't work out as I had hoped." His eyes were bleak, and for a moment he didn't continue. Rose wondered if he had ever considered his son in his plans.

"Didn't you like Colorado?" Rose persisted.

"It was stimulating to be in on the birth of a state, but Colorado wasn't kind to me at first. I had invested heavily in a gold mine that wasn't any good, and I lost most of the money I'd taken with me. I had to start over again, and I had a rough time of it. With a lot of hard work and determination,

I finally achieved my goal."

Again he paused, and sadness filled his eyes. Perhaps his lack of money had kept him from returning to see about his son. Would Martin consider his father's loss of fortune as sufficient reason to justify ten years of neglect?

"But when I found out that success wasn't enough for contentment, I decided to leave." His face brightened, and he said, "Forgive me for talking about my own affairs. I'd rather talk about you."

"You needn't apologize. I asked about your life in Colorado. I haven't traveled like you have, so I don't have much to say. Most of my life has been spent on the waterfront of Louisville, except for the summers when Gramps traveled up and down the Ohio and other Kentucky rivers. Mostly he fishes for a living. He has standing orders for fish in the hotels and restaurants in Louisville. He even catches frogs for some of the more elite restaurants. When he travels in the summer, he stocks the boat with dishes and tin household items. He also has pottery to sell. He's done all kinds of things during his lifetime."

"Forgive me for saying this, but you seem to be a poised, educated woman. How did you manage that if you spent your life on the river?"

"My parents died when I was a child, so my grandparents took me in. Gramps and Granny love the life they lead, but they wanted something better for me. Granny worked six years as a cook and housekeeper at Miss Bordeaux's Academy to pay for my education."

"That was commendable of them."

Noticing the compassion in Edward's eyes, Rose was taken aback. She quickly regained her composure and continued. "I suppose so, but I didn't enjoy those years. I was out of place at Miss Bordeaux's, and most of the girls didn't let me forget that I was the granddaughter of the cook. Miss Bordeaux didn't show favorites, and she wouldn't tolerate any persecution, but she wasn't around all the time. Now that I'm older, I appreciate the sacrifice Granny made for me."

"Her sacrifice doesn't seem to have been in vain. You seem to have done very well for yourself."

"I wouldn't be living where I do now if a good friend of our family hadn't left his estate to me when he died. He and Gramps had been friends since he came from New York when I was just a child."

"He didn't have any family?"

"Not unless he had some in New York. If he did, he didn't talk about them."

"It sounds as if both of us have had similar experiences— having to make our own way in life. I didn't enjoy my struggles in Colorado, either, but I'm glad that I stuck with it. Although I realize now that I've missed some of the more important things in life."

Edward paused in his story. *Is he lost in thoughts of the past, or is he thinking about the future?* Rose wondered.

"Tell me something about Louisville, Miss Thurston."

"If you don't think it's too forward of me, you can call me by my given name as everybody else does. It's Rose."

"It would be my pleasure. Rose is a pretty name."

"My parents were landlubbers, as Gramps said. My mother didn't like traveling on the river, and she married a man who worked on land. I was born the first day of June, and Granny said my mother looked out the window at a white rambler rose on their porch and chose my name. I like it, too."

"I got my name from my father," he said. "Now about Louisville?"

"Gramps is the one to tell you about Louisville, Mr. Moody."

He touched her hand. "Edward."

"Talk to my grandpa, Edward. He came here with his parents after the close of the War of 1812. His parents floated downriver on a flatboat. Louisville has been home to the Thurstons ever since. He has some wild stories of the Indian wars and the War Between the States."

It was dark when they finished dinner, and Edward said, "I'd prefer to see you home. I don't want you going alone in the dark."

"Thank you, but I won't be alone." She checked the watch on the chain around her neck. "My coachman is supposed to pick me up, and I'm sure he'll be waiting. You may walk to the carriage with me. That way you will know I'm well protected."

Edward held the door open for her, and she walked down the steps before him. Isaiah was waiting at the curb, as she knew he would be.

"Mr. Moody, this is Isaiah Taylor. He'll take me home."

Edward looked at her, surprise on his face. It wasn't customary for ladies to even acknowledge the presence of their servants, but this faux pas convinced him even more that Rose Thurston was a unique person who made her own rules for living.

The coachman had his hat brim pulled low on his forehead, and his face was obscure in the dimly lit street. "Good evening, Isaiah," Edward said, and Isaiah lifted his hand in greeting. Edward turned to Rose. "Will I see you again?"

"That depends on how long you stay in Louisville."

"I don't know how long my business will take, or how successful it will be. I will contact you before I leave."

He handed her up into the carriage. "Thank you for dinner."

Rose could feel his intense brown eyes following them as Isaiah pulled away from the curb.

"Does he know anything?" Isaiah asked when they were out of hearing.

"Apparently not, but he's a highly determined, intelligent man, and I have a feeling that when he sets his eye on a goal, he works to get it. I'm worried, Isaiah."

"No use borrowing trouble, Miss Rose."

three

Edward enjoyed a better night's sleep than he had had for months. He wakened to the sounds of Louisville starting its day—steamboat whistles, the voices of hotel workers, and a cleaning crew sweeping the streets. His thoughts turned immediately to Rose Thurston. His companions for years had been primarily men, and he'd forgotten how pleasurable it was to sit at a candlelit table, across from a beautiful woman, and enjoy a leisurely meal.

He shook himself into reality. He had an important reason for coming to Louisville, and he must not let his interest in Rose deter him from his search. He tugged the rope beside his bed, and soon a porter answered his summons. He asked for hot water, and when the man returned, Edward questioned him. "Where can I rent a carriage for the day?"

"There's a barn two blocks down Main Street where you can hire carriages by the day or the week," the porter answered. "Business is down a little now because the high water has slowed the river traffic. I doubt you'll have any trouble renting a carriage."

After he dressed and had breakfast, Edward went to the barn and was soon outfitted with a buggy and a horse. He asked the hostler directions to cemeteries in town and wrote down the names and directions. Cave Hill Cemetery was the farthest away, but apparently the largest cemetery, so he decided to start his search there.

Accustomed to speedy western horses, Edward was disgusted with the old nag that pulled his carriage. But the plodding pace gave Edward plenty of time to survey the city. In addition to the river traffic, several railroad lines crisscrossed the town. Captain Parsons had told him that Louisville had a population of more than 160,000. Before he turned on Broadway, which he would follow to the cemetery, Edward passed through a section of town containing majestic houses of varied types of architecture. He drove along Third Street, wondering which of those homes belonged to Rose Thurston.

Apparently Louisville had not suffered much damage during the Civil War, for the homes looked as if they had been standing for many years. Tulips and daffodils bloomed in the lawns he passed.

Searching for his wife's grave would probably be like looking for a needle in a haystack. Edward had provided enough money for a headstone, but for all he knew, those people on the shanty boat might have kept it for themselves. He squirmed uncomfortably when he considered that Martha might have been buried in a pauper's grave. But his conscience pointed out that it would be his fault if she were. If he had stayed behind to arrange for Martha's burial and to provide for the welfare of his child, he would have been too late to have sunk his money in a worthless mine. God had given him warning signs all along the way, but he had been too stubborn to heed them.

Edward pulled the horse to a stop when he reached the cemetery and paused, wondering which of the many curved, hilly roads he should take. Stone mausoleums and towering marble shafts indicated that Louisville's elite citizens had been buried in this cemetery. He turned toward smaller, less majestic stones—believing that he might find Martha's grave. He judged that the cemetery covered more than a hundred acres, and it would be impossible for him to locate his wife's grave unless he found a caretaker.

After driving for fifteen or twenty minutes, Edward decided to return to town and visit the cemetery office the hostler had mentioned to him. Undoubtedly they would have records of burials. Before turning back, he saw a man working a short distance away. If he was the caretaker he might be able to provide the information Edward needed. He doubted that the horse would move from the spot if he left it unfettered, but he tied the animal to the trunk of a large elm tree. Edward walked toward the worker, who was kneeling on the ground, smoothing the soil over a grave with a trowel. He had a pail of grass seed beside him. He didn't look up when Edward stopped beside him but continued with his work.

"Mawnin', sir," the man said.

"Good morning," Edward replied. "I'm a stranger here, and I wonder if you might provide some information."

"Happy to oblige if I can, sir." The man's voice sounded familiar, but all of the natives spoke in a similar drawl.

"I'm looking for the grave of Martha Moody. I don't know whether the grave is even marked, or even if she's buried in this cemetery."

"You won't have no trouble findin' that grave." The man looked up briefly and pointed to a burial plot marked by a marble angel, several yards away.

"That looks like a new stone."

"Yes, sir—put up a few weeks ago."

"Thanks for your help," Edward said.

Puzzled, Edward walked quickly toward the grave. Martha had died ten years ago—why was the stone new?

The grave was well tended. The expensive stone had a bouquet of flowers at its base. The petals were turning brown around the edges, so they had been brought a few days ago. Who would have placed the stone? Martha had a sister in Pittsburgh. Had she and her husband located the grave and marked it? He turned, hoping the caretaker could solve the puzzle for him, but the man had disappeared. Where could he have gone so quickly?

Edward knelt by the grave, but he felt no emotion at all. Had the years diminished his love for Martha? He had thought that he would love her forever, but living with a memory for ten years must have stifled any feelings he held for her.

Edward returned to the carriage and stepped into it, but he didn't take up the reins immediately. How could he learn who had been caring for Martha's grave? Who could tell him if his son was alive? He had learned long ago that to solve a puzzle he often had to go back to the beginning.

He vaguely remembered the shanty boat where his wife had died and the two women he had seen. Since residents on shanty boats were nomadic people, it wasn't likely that they would still be living in Louisville, but perhaps the man who owned the shanty that they had rescued might know something to further his search. And Rose Thurston had lived on a shanty boat. Perhaps she could help him. He wished he had asked her last night, but while he talked with Rose, Edward had forgotten his mission in Louisville. He picked up the reins, flicked them several times, and finally the nag moved to his commands. He headed toward the waterfront.

❧

Rose stood in the backyard, leaning on the wooden fence, watching Martin ride Tibbets around the paddock. Although Martin had always been hesitant to try new things, he didn't seem to have any qualms about riding the pony. His friend, Cam Miller, a year older than Martin, had had a pony for several months, and Cam sometimes let Martin ride.

Rose stepped backward out of Martin's hearing when Isaiah loped into the yard. He slid out of the saddle and sauntered toward her.

"You had Mr. Moody figgered out, Miss Rose. I found out from the hostler that Mr. Moody had hired a horse and carriage, and that he had asked about graveyards. The hostler thought he was going to Cave Hill Cemetery. I took a few shortcuts and got there before he did. I was real busy workin' when he came. He asked about the grave, and as soon as I told him where it was, I got out of sight. He seemed mournful about his wife's death, and he sure acted puzzled about that new stone."

"What did he do then?"

"He didn't stay long, but he headed back in the direction of the hotel. I rustled on home."

"Thanks, Isaiah," Rose said, her eyes on Martin.

"You worried, Miss Rose?" Isaiah asked.

She nodded. "Yes, I am. I suppose it shows a lack of faith, but I am worried."

"But the boy is yours, all tight and legal, ain't he?"

"That's true, but I want to do what's best for Martin. Maybe he needs a father now more than he needs a mother."

"It'll come out right, Miss Rose."

"I hope so. Now that you're back to watch Martin, I'm going inside."

"Let me know if you want me to do anything else."

❧

After Edward turned in the horse and carriage, he ate a light lunch at the hotel before he started out again. The river had fallen a foot or two during the night, but he still walked through a few inches of mud to reach his destination. A thin filter of smoke rose from a rusty piece of stovepipe on the *Vagabond*'s roof. The proprietor sat on the deck of the boat, dangling a fish line in the murky water.

Edward had heard this man's name when he'd boarded the *Mary Ann* a few nights ago, and he cast around in his mind trying to remember it. "Mr. Thurston," he said tentatively. When the man didn't correct him, he decided he had remembered correctly.

"Come on over, Mr. Moody. Lottie, bring our guest a cup of coffee!" he shouted.

"No, thank you," Edward said. "I dined before I left the hotel." He walked across the gangplank, wondering how Thurston knew his name.

Harry jerked his line, and a large catfish landed beside Edward's feet. Harry removed it from the line, dropped the fish into a tub of water, and put another worm on his hook before he gave any more attention to Edward.

"Sit down, Mr. Moody," he said, motioning to a rocking chair. "What's on your mind?"

"Have you lived in this area very long?"

"I was born on a shanty and have lived on one ever since. In the summer, me and my family travel the rivers, but Louisville is our winter port."

Edward squirmed in his chair. "Then you probably know most of the shanty people in this area."

Harry wiggled his fishing hook. "Why don't you speak what's on your mind, Mr. Moody? What do you want to know?"

Edward still hesitated. Would he be wiser to continue on to Pittsburgh or to return to Colorado, without resurrecting the past? Did he really want to know what had happened to his child?

"Ten years ago, my wife died in childbirth on a shanty boat in this area. I went to the cemetery today. There was a new headstone on my wife's grave. I want some information about the people who took care of my wife, and I'm curious why this new stone has been placed on her grave recently. I left money for these details to be seen to then."

"That bag of money wasn't all you left behind, was it, Mr. Moody?" a woman's voice asked.

Edward turned and looked at the woman standing in the doorway. He stood up to acknowledge her presence, and she waved him back into the chair. She held a leather bag, which she handed to him.

"A stone was put on your wife's grave. The money left after we bought the stone was put in a bank, where it's been drawing interest. The receipt is in the bag. We didn't use nary cent of your money for ourselves."

"You. . . You're the one who took care of my wife?" he stuttered. "There was only one grave at the cemetery. Did my son survive?"

"Yes. We saved your money for the boy to have when he became a man, but the child don't need it now."

Edward glanced around the humble shelter these people called home, marveling that they hadn't used any of the money that was rightfully theirs.

"But the new tombstone! You should keep the money to pay for that."

"The marker we put up crumbled away. The new stone was put there a few weeks ago by our granddaughter. We didn't pay for it."

"Where is my son?"

Lottie and Harry exchanged glances. "Our granddaughter has him."

"Wait a minute," Edward said, slowly comprehending. "There was a woman and a boy on this boat yesterday. Was that. . . ?"

Harry nodded.

"But why didn't you tell me?"

"Why should we?" Lottie said. "You abandoned the boy once. We weren't about to tell him who you were until we knew your intentions."

"I returned to Kentucky to discover if my son survived. Does he live on this boat?"

"Not now. He's living with our granddaughter on Third Street. Go to the top of the bank and follow Main Street till you come to Third. Anybody can point out the house to you."

"Is your granddaughter Rose Thurston?" Edward demanded loudly, a shadow of anger flashing across his face. "I had dinner with her last night. If she knew who I was, why didn't she tell me?"

"Maybe she wanted to size you up to see what kind of man you are. I hate to say it, Mr. Moody, but you didn't make much of an impression on us the last time we saw you."

"I had just lost my wife. I was overcome with grief. What did you expect?"

"I'm not judgin' you one way or another, Mr. Moody—just answerin' your questions," Lottie said.

Edward felt betrayed. He had liked Rose more than any other woman he'd known since he had married Martha. She had seemed to enjoy their time together last night. Why had she deceived him?

Edward stood up. "I'll go see her then. She told me she lived in the Boardman House. Does she have the boy with her?"

Harry yanked another catfish out of the water. "Yes, sir. She's been lookin' after him ever since the night you gave your boy to her."

Edward felt his face flushing, whether from anger or embarrassment he didn't know. Without speaking, he dropped the money bag on the rocking chair and walked off the deck of the *Vagabond*. It was obvious that reclaiming his son might prove to be difficult.

He walked rapidly to Third Street, and after a few blocks, he asked an old gentleman who was working in his yard to direct him to Rose Thurston's house. The man pointed across the street to a three-story stone-faced house. He marched toward the house with a determined stride.

❧

Rose saw Edward Moody coming toward her home. She turned from the window and walked into the dining room, where Sallie was working. "Will you answer the door? I want to put this off as long as I can. I'll go upstairs until you let him in."

Pausing on the first step of the back stairway, she inquired, "Is Martin still out in the paddock?"

"Yes. He's gonna grow to that pony if he stays on it much longer."

With a faint smile Rose said, "The new will wear off before long."

She went into her bedroom, tense, but excited, too. She dreaded this meeting. Perhaps she should have told Edward last night, but she had enjoyed his company so much that she didn't want to spoil their time together. She had a feeling that their amicability of the night before was about to cease. She looked in the mirror. She wasn't dressed as stylishly as the previous evening, but she still looked all right in her plain linen dress, with only one petticoat, and the hem a few inches from the floor.

When Rose moved to Third Street, she had adopted the dress of the society ladies of the town, more for Martin than herself. She was much more comfortable in the homemade dresses that Lottie had made for her, but she didn't want Martin to be ashamed of her appearance. Only a few neighbors had offered any overtures of friendship, and Rose hadn't asked for any favors. To them, she was still the shanty boat girl. For herself, she didn't mind, but she hoped that time would remove the stigma of the early years of poverty from Martin's life.

"Company, Miss Rose," Sallie called from the entrance hall.

Rose leaned against the doorframe and closed her eyes.

Help me, God. Give me the wisdom to handle this situation.

❧

Edward sat on an upholstered sofa while he waited for Rose. He forced himself to take in his surroundings in an attempt to calm his demeanor. He couldn't help but admire the wide entrance hall that stretched the width of the building. A red carpet covered the floor, and along the walls were massive cabinets, holding marble and porcelain articles that Edward recognized as products of Europe. The wide walnut stairway stretched upward for three stories.

He stood when he heard Rose's steps. His indignation, unsuccessfully calmed by the beautiful furnishings, melted at the sight of Rose Thurston descending the staircase. She was as striking in daylight as she had been in the candlelit dining room the night before. She was of medium height with a trim figure. Her bronze-gold hair swept upward from her slender, graceful neck. When she stopped on the bottom step, he noticed that her dark blue eyes were framed by thick, dark lashes, which hadn't been apparent in the shadowy dining room last night.

But her beauty did not quell his anger for long as he again remembered the girl who had been present when his wife had died. The years had erased any memory of the appearance of the girl who had assisted in the delivery of his child. But he had never forgotten her accusation that *he* was responsible for the death of his wife. The thought of her unjust words had rankled for years. He stepped forward and greeted her with a slight bow.

&

As Rose stood before Edward, the cold expression in his brown eyes brought a chill, but she spoke as pleasantly as possible, under the circumstances. "What can I do for you this afternoon?"

"I've been to see your grandparents."

Since Isaiah had continued to follow Edward's movements, Rose was aware of his visit to the *Vagabond*. She had expected him to call, for her few encounters with him had convinced her that he was a man of action. She had a feeling that Edward wouldn't delay once he decided on a course to take.

"Please come into the parlor," she said. She strolled toward a room to her left—a long room with two entrances. A walnut fireplace dominated one wall, a mahogany grand piano stood in one corner and tables of various dark woods were scattered throughout. The room was furnished with beautiful, upholstered matching loveseats and chairs. Rose sat down and motioned Edward into a seat opposite hers.

"I suppose you know why I'm here," he said as he sat stiffly on the chair.

"Of course," she said.

Sallie entered with a teapot, cups, and a plate of cookies on a tray. She put it on the table between them. Rose thanked her, and Sallie gave her a reassuring smile before returning to the kitchen.

Rose poured a cup of tea and handed it to Edward, then took a cup for herself. She needed it. She was far more apprehensive than she wanted to be.

"Why didn't you tell me last night that we had met ten years ago?"

"I recognized you immediately on the *Mary Ann*," Rose said. "And when I accepted your invitation to dinner, I hadn't decided whether or not to tell you who I was. But I enjoyed the evening, and I didn't want to spoil it by introducing a subject that might lead to controversy."

"I've wondered for years if my son survived, but the pressure of business kept me in Colorado. I came back to discover what happened to him. I want to thank you for caring for him."

"It has been a pleasure."

"And for looking after my wife's grave. The stone is a fine one. I intend to pay you for it."

She shook her head. "No. I did that for Martin."

"Martin?"

"That was as close as I could come to Martha—his mother's name. His full name is Martin Moody Thurston—the name I put on the papers when I adopted him."

"Adopted him?"

"Yes, seven years ago when he was three years old."

"You had no right to adopt him without my permission."

Rose placed her teacup on the table and walked around the room before returning to her seat. The tension in the room had erased the camaraderie they had enjoyed temporarily.

"Do I have to remind you, Mr. Moody," she began, reverting to the formal use of his name, "that I tried to give your child to you when you rushed away from the *Vagabond* ten years ago? I remember your exact words. 'I don't want him—you keep him.'"

Edward lowered his head. "Those words have haunted me for years."

"And," Rose continued relentlessly, "*if* you were so interested in your son, why haven't you contacted him during these years? It hasn't been easy to explain to the child why his father didn't want him."

Last night Rose had seemed so feminine and amenable. Today he saw a determined side of her personality. "Am I going to be allowed to see him?" Edward said.

"As far as I'm concerned you may see him, but don't expect any filial affection. You're a stranger to him."

"So you've turned him against me?"

Trying to control her temper, Rose said, "To the contrary. I've taken him regularly to visit his mother's grave so he would have a sense of being her son. For several years I was able to convince him that you were probably unable to come back to see him. As he's grown older, he's made a few decisions on his own. If he wants to see you, I have no objections."

Rose stood again. "Sallie," she called. Judging by the speed with which Sallie entered the parlor, Rose knew she had listened to every word they had said. "Is Martin still in the paddock?"

"He finished ridin' the pony and is headin' this way now."

"Ask him to come here for a little while, please."

In a few minutes, Martin hurried into the room and threw himself at his mother. "I love Tibbetts, Mama. He's the best birthday present I've ever had."

Rose smoothed his straw-colored hair, and taking a handkerchief from her pocket, she wiped dusty spots from his face. His sparkling blue eyes took in their visitor, and he sidled closer to Rose.

Edward rose to his feet, as if on the strings of a marionette. "Martha's eyes," he mumbled.

"I didn't know we had company," Martin said.

Rose gripped his hand tightly. She couldn't think of an easy way to break the news. "Martin, this is your father, Edward Moody."

Edward held out his hand. "Hello, Martin." He wasn't prepared for the expressive anger spreading over Martin's face or for the vitriolic gleam in his blue eyes.

Martin slapped away the hand that was held out to him. "So you haven't been dead or bad sick as Mama and me thought you might be. You just didn't care anything about me. Well, I don't want to see *you* now." He raced out of the parlor, and his steps sounded on the stairs.

Rose clasped her hands to stop their shaking and mentally cautioned herself to be unconcerned about the hurt, lost look on Edward's face. "As far as I'm concerned," she said quietly, "you have your answer, Mr. Moody."

four

Edward started after Martin, but Rose blocked the way. He turned on her as angrily as Martin had defied him. In spite of the trauma of the moment, Rose felt like laughing. *Like father, like son.* For the most part, Martin had been an amiable child and had seldom lost his temper. But she was amazed at how his few childish fits of anger were reminiscent of his father's sullen looks.

"You've turned the boy against me," he accused.

The door of Martin's bedroom slammed. Refusing to take offense at Edward's words, Rose ordered quietly, "Sit down, Mr. Moody." When he sulkily obeyed, she posed, "Do you realize how ridiculous it is for you to appear out of the blue and expect the child to cozy up to you? If not, you don't know much about children."

"I know nothing about children."

"I didn't either until Martin came into my life. In spite of your accusation, I have never tried to usurp the place of Martin's natural parents. I've kept the memory of his mother alive in his heart and, as much as possible, have tried to shield him from the fact that you abandoned him. But he's an intelligent, sensitive boy, and as the years passed and you didn't return, he came to his own conclusions."

Edward seemed to deflate before her eyes. "I know that you are right. If you hadn't taken good care of my son, he no doubt would have died. I do appreciate the care you've given the child, and I hope I can make amends for my churlish behavior."

Rose nodded her acceptance of his thanks.

"But that still doesn't change the fact that he's my son—my

heir, and I want him now. I've accumulated a good deal of money in the past few years, and I can give the boy more advantages than you can."

With a smile, Rose glanced around the spacious, well-appointed room. "Oh, I don't know. A year ago, I might have agreed with you, but not now. And I've given him ten years of love and devotion. To you, he's just a possession."

"I do love him."

Rose lifted her eyebrows. "After seeing him for less than five minutes, how can you say that? Love comes slowly."

Without comment on her statement, Edward continued, "And I mean to have your adoption set aside. No judge in the land will deny my rights."

"Edward," Rose said, "I don't want to be your enemy. I believe that we both want what is best for Martin. I love him enough that if he wants to go with you, after he's learned to know you, I'll give him up. But you're a stranger to him. Can't you understand that you have to earn the child's love and trust? What are your plans for him, if you should get custody?"

Shamefaced, Edward admitted, "Actually, I haven't made any. I really thought the child had died, but I had to see for myself."

"Now that you know he is alive, you had better approach this matter realistically. Let's say I agreed to turn Martin over to you. What would you do with a ten-year-old boy? Would you take him away from the only family he's ever known? Aren't you concerned for his happiness at all? Don't you want what's best for him?"

Edward stood and threw his arms wide with uncertainty. He then left the room and walked out of the house without any comment.

Although Rose had exhibited a composed front to Edward, as soon as she heard the door close behind him, she slumped in the chair and buried her face in her hands. Sallie came into the room and knelt beside her mistress.

"Did you hear everything, Sallie?"

"Yes, ma'am. Do you think he can take the boy?"

Rose shook her head. "I don't know. It worries me."

"Now the good Lord helped you and your Granny save that boy from dyin' when he was a baby. He ain't about to let that man take him away from you."

Rose took Sallie's work-hardened hand. "Thanks, my friend. I'll never let him go unless I feel sure that it's to Martin's advantage to be with his father. He doesn't seem like a bad man."

"But a selfish one, I figger," Sallie said.

"I'm not sure of that, either. I truly believe he could be a good father, and Martin is at the age when he needs some male guidance. I've often wondered if I can cope with Martin's needs as he gets older."

"Don't borrow trouble. I'll bring you a fresh cup of tea. That'll make you feel better."

Sighing, Rose said, "No, I need to talk to Martin. And I don't know what to say."

"The Lord Jesus will give you the right words."

With leaden feet, Rose climbed the massive walnut stairway. She expected Martin to be facedown on his bed, but he stood beside the window, watching his father walk away from their home. Rose knelt beside him.

"I don't like him," Martin said stubbornly.

Even after ten years, Rose still didn't know how to deal with Martin's moods. She supposed it took a lifetime to know how to bring up a child. She looked at him closely, but Martin apparently hadn't shed a tear.

"Maybe it's too soon to say that. You only saw him a few minutes."

"Why'd he have to come back now?"

"He said he came to find out what had happened to you."

Edward had disappeared from sight now, and Martin turned to look Rose full in the face. "Do you believe that?"

Rose hesitated, but remembering the stricken look on Edward's face when Martin had rejected him, she answered slowly, "Yes. Yes, I believe it."

"Well, I don't."

"Don't worry about it now. I'll have Sallie bring up some hot water so you can take a bath. You smell like Tibbets."

A grin brightened his face. "I like *him*."

&

The next day, after inquiring from the hotel clerk about Louisville's lawyers, Edward went to the office of Duncan McKee on Jefferson Street. A portly man, probably in his fifties, McKee had an office in the rear wing of his antebellum home.

After McKee greeted Edward and ushered him into a square, high-ceilinged room, he asked, "Are you a stranger to Louisville, Mr. Moody?"

"I recently arrived from Colorado."

"And why do you need my services? Are you planning to settle in our city?"

"That depends," Edward said. He hesitated, hardly knowing what to say. Was he making the right move? He wanted his boy, but on the other hand he hated to cause Rose Thurston any trouble. He was obligated to her for caring for his wife's grave and giving Martin a good home. Besides, the woman interested him—the first time he had looked upon any female with interest since the death of his wife. It was a strange feeling, and he didn't know how to account for it.

Briefly he explained to McKee about the death of his wife, his grief at her death, and why he couldn't take the child with him at that time.

The lawyer lifted his hand. "Just a minute. Is Martin Thurston your son?"

"Yes. I came back to Louisville to find him. Rose Thurston told me she has adopted him. Since I'm the child's father, and I didn't give permission for that adoption, I don't believe it is legal. I want you to represent me in overturning that adoption."

McKee's lips twisted into a cynical smile. "For ten years, you haven't made any effort to find out what had happened to your son?"

Martin felt his face getting warm. "I've had a difficult ten years, Mr. McKee. I suppose, as you grow older, you get wiser. I eventually prospered, but I realized that my money was *all* I had. Although I feared my boy had died, I had never forgotten him. For years I didn't have the courage to find out. I know I'm not without blame, but it's never too late to correct past mistakes."

"I'll represent you in this situation, Mr. Moody, and I'll give you the best representation possible. However, it's only fair to warn you that you're facing an uphill battle, probably a losing one."

"What can you tell me about Miss Thurston?"

McKee moved papers around on his desk and picked up a pencil, which he turned in his hands as he spoke. "If you think you can take the child because of Miss Thurston's reputation, you don't have any case. The Thurstons are poor people, and Rose lived most of her life on her grandparents' shanty boat. In summertime, the Thurstons are nomads. They are poor. Harry fishes and does other river-related things to keep his family going. But as far as character, you'll not find a blot against Rose Thurston or her grandparents."

"She has never married?"

"No. As far as I know, she has never been interested in any man. She has devoted her life to rearing *your* son, working hard to provide a good education for him. She did that before she had any money."

"I left some gold coins behind that they could have used, but they spent only enough to pay for my wife's burial. They banked the rest of the money for Martin."

McKee laughed and amusement gleamed in his eyes. "I forgot to mention that the Thurstons are proud people."

Edward's conscience hammered that the honorable decision

was to leave Louisville and not interfere in his son's life, but he couldn't accept that. He wanted his son, and he knew that he had another reason now for staying in Louisville. But if he tried to force the custody battle against Rose, what would that do to their personal relationship?

Believing that his child's welfare had to come before his own emotional feelings, he said, "Then you will take my case?"

"Give me a few days to study the legalities while you consider if you're sure you want to involve yourself in a lawsuit."

"Will you tell me how Rose Thurston got her money?"

"Yes, since it isn't any secret. It's a rag-to-riches story and a fairy tale all rolled into one. John Boardman came here from New York soon after the War Between the States ended. He traveled through this area when he was a soldier in the Union Army, and he liked the Ohio River system. When the war ended, he moved to Kentucky. He invested his money in the river industry and became prosperous. A few years ago he built the large home where Rose lives."

"It's strange architecture."

McKee nodded agreement. "And not to my liking—I prefer the columned houses of the 1840s, but John was something of an innovator. He didn't pattern himself after others."

"Rose said he left the house to her, but I didn't know a large fortune went with it. What's the connection between Boardman and the Thurstons?"

McKee narrowed his eyes, and Edward thought he had offended him. He hadn't meant to imply that the relationship was improper. He opened his mouth to explain, but McKee continued.

"About eight years ago, John had the *Silver Queen* built. That showboat was his pride and joy, and he spent a few enjoyable summers taking it up and down the Ohio and on Kentucky's smaller rivers. In spite of his love for the river,

John had never learned to swim. In fact, he was afraid of the water."

McKee paused, and Edward was conscious of the quietness in the room—only the ticking of a mantel clock could be heard.

"Early one morning, Boardman went fishing in a johnboat. He was out in the middle of the river when the boat sprung a leak. He panicked and called for help, but it was a Sunday morning and no one was working around the wharf. He was twenty or thirty feet from shore, but Rose Thurston heard him calling. Rose learned to swim practically before she could walk. She dived into the water and caught John before he went under for the last time.

"In his fear, he tried to fight Rose. She hit him on the jaw and knocked him out. She didn't have any trouble towing him to safety after that."

McKee was a vivid storyteller, and Edward envisioned the scene—a frightened man hindering the girl who was trying to save him. "I suppose Mr. Boardman was grateful and gave her the house."

"Not right away. I told you the Thurstons are proud people. They wouldn't take anything from John. But he never forgot. He made out a will and left everything he had to Rose. He included a note in the will, which she was to read after his death. He pleaded with her to take his estate; 'If not for yourself, think of the boy.' Although Rose was happy with her life as it was and didn't want to leave the river, she sacrificed her way of life to raise Martin in the manner she suspected was his birthright."

"How do you know all of this?"

"I'm the one who wrote John Boardman's will."

"Then I take it you would side with Rose in this adoption matter."

"Take it any way you want to," McKee said shortly. "If I take your case, I'll give you the best representation possible.

I'm just warning you to consider your options before you sue for custody of Martin Thurston. You may lose not only your money, but any chance to reconcile with your son."

"What other way is there?"

A crooked grin curved McKee's mouth. "You're a grown man, Mr. Moody. Give it some thought."

Bewildered by the man's manner, Edward replied slowly, "Thank you—I will."

≈

Again, Rose set Isaiah to watch Edward's movements. He reported that Edward had gone to Duncan McKee's office and had spent an hour there. Over the next three days, Edward had hired a carriage and toured Louisville and the surrounding countryside. Each day, he had stopped by the cemetery to spend some time at his wife's grave. One day, Edward had walked to the schoolhouse, stood in the shadow of a building across the street, and watched as Martin left school to go home. He had made no effort to speak to the boy. Another day, he had spent several hours at the waterfront, looking over the Boardman boats, especially the *Silver Queen*.

Rose knew that Edward must have learned about her inheritance, and she thanked God for John Boardman's generosity. If she were still living on the *Vagabond* with Martin, Edward would have a major reason to take the child. It was comforting to know that if it came to a court battle, she had the money to hire a lawyer.

Rose couldn't get Edward Moody out of her mind, and it annoyed her that her preoccupation concerned Edward as a man more than as Martin's father. Lying awake at night, she thought of his generous mouth, displaying straight, white teeth, his deep-timbred voice, and his vivid, intelligent eyes. She considered his powerful, muscular body. In spite of his size, Edward moved quickly and gracefully.

Edward's obvious unhappiness troubled her. Most of the time, his expression was serious and somewhat lonely. There was a sense of isolation about the man that made her feel sorry for him. He must have spent ten lonely years without either his wife or son. But when his rare smile flashed across his face, her pulses raced, and she was hard put to remember what trouble this man could cause her.

$\approx$

During the days of exploring Louisville and its environs, Edward pondered the lawyer's comment that he was a grown man and that there was another way to get his son besides going to court. Mr. McKee had apparently known Rose Thurston for years, so surely he hadn't steered him in the wrong direction. But had he misunderstood the lawyer's meaning?

After a week of indecision, Martin made one more visit to Cave Hill Cemetery. He knelt by his wife's grave. Rather than praying, he talked to his wife as if she were beside him.

"Martha, when I married you, I thought I would always love you. For the past few years, I've been in love with a memory. Now I can hardly remember what you looked like. I had thought that if our son still lived, he would remind me of you. But, except for his eyes, I see only my features on his face. I feel guilty to even think of taking another wife, but I'm doing it for our son. I can't raise the child alone. Please forgive me for the step I'm about to take."

Once he made the decision, Edward didn't delay. He returned the carriage to the barn. He wrote a note to Rose and asked the hotel clerk to have it delivered. After he received a positive answer from Rose, Edward went to his room and dressed with care. He chose a gray broadcloth suit that he had purchased a few months before he left Denver. His vest was of black silk, and a splash of red in his tie relieved the somber colors.

As he walked toward the Thurston home, he noticed a florist's shop, and believing that this occasion warranted flowers, he stepped inside.

"I'd like to buy a bouquet for a special occasion. What do you have available?"

"We have a recent shipment of rosebuds," the florist said. "I can arrange some mixed rosebuds for a reasonable price."

"Cost isn't an issue. I'll take a dozen roses."

Edward was pleased with the man's arrangements—red, white, and yellow rosebuds arranged in a crystal vase. He inhaled the sweet scents of the flowers as he continued toward the Thurston home. He had watched to be sure that Martin had gone to school this morning. He believed he could deal better with Rose if Martin wasn't there.

❧

Rose had been in the parlor picking at the keys of the grand piano when Sallie had entered with Edward's note. She took the message from the envelope and scanned it quickly. Puzzled, she glanced at Sallie. She then read the message aloud. " 'Miss Thurston, I request the pleasure of calling on you at two o'clock this afternoon. Your servant, Edward Moody.' " She asked Sallie, "What do you think this means?"

Sallie's eyes widened. "Nothing good, I'll bet. The hotel messenger is waiting for an answer."

"Well, why not," Rose said. "If he wants me to refuse his request again, that's up to him."

She went into the small room adjacent to the back porch that John Boardman had used for his office. Picking up a pen, she dipped it in the inkwell.

I'll be home this afternoon at two o'clock, she wrote on a note card. She put the card in an envelope and sealed the flap with wax. She took it to the man waiting in the foyer and gave him a coin for his services.

She looked at the Chippendale clock on the mantel in the parlor. She had three hours to wait for her guest. She wasn't hungry, but when noon came, she sat at the small kitchen table to eat a bowl of soup. "Sit down and keep me company, Sallie."

Sallie scolded Rose for her lack of propriety in fraternizing with the servants. Rose replied as she always did, "You can take the girl off the shanty boat, but you can't take the shanty boat out of the girl. I'm trying for Martin's sake, but I'll never enjoy this way of life. Give me a fishing pole and a can of worms, and I can be happy all day sitting on the *Vagabond*'s deck. I'm at loose ends in this house when you do all of the work. That's why I'm trying to learn how to play the piano. I need something to occupy my time."

"You sounded pretty good this morning. I recognized 'Yankee Doodle' and 'Dixie.' "

"I learned to play Gramps's banjo before I was twelve, so I ought to be able to master the piano. We'll see."

"What are you going to wear this afternoon?" Sallie asked.

Rose glanced down at her blue-striped dress with its tight-fitting bodice and pleated skirt, short enough to show the toes of her black kid shoes. "What's wrong with this? It was clean when I put it on this morning."

"You always look good, Miss Rose. I just thought you might want to fix up for Mr. Moody," Sallie added slyly.

Rose glanced at her, wondering at the amused look on Sallie's face. She flipped her hair, which she had tied back with a small scarf when she'd gotten up. "If you have time, you can fix my hair. I wasn't expecting to have company today, so I just brushed it and let it hang loose."

After Sallie finished with her hair, Rose still had an hour to wait. If she were honest with herself, Rose knew she wanted Edward Moody to see her at her best, and not just because of Martin, either. She viewed her appearance in the floor-length mirror at the foot of the steps, seeing her lady of the manor pose, not the shanty boat girl. To quiet her nerves, Rose played on the piano until she heard the doorknocker. She swung around on the stool as Sallie walked down the hall. Sallie winked at her, her white teeth gleaming. Soon she ushered Edward into the parlor.

"I'll bring some tea after while, Miss Rose."

With a wide smile and a little bow, she left the room. When they weren't alone, Sallie was careful to act the part of a servant.

"I heard the piano," Edward said. "Were you playing?"

Rose's eyes revealed her amusement. "If you listen very long, you'll know I can't play. But I'm trying to learn. It will be helpful if I have to play the calliope on the showboat this summer."

He handed her the vase of roses.

"How nice of you. Thank you." She set the flowers on a table beside the door. "Sit down," she invited and waited for him to speak.

"Rose," he said. "I'll come to the point. This is difficult for me to say, but I hope you will hear me out."

He looked at her expectantly, but she remained silent.

"I've decided that you and I share a common problem. If we work together, instead of considering ourselves enemies, I think we can avoid any difficulties."

Her eyes narrowed, and she spoke stiffly. "So far I've had no reason to consider you as an enemy. Don't give me one."

Edward blundered on, ignoring the gathering storm clouds in the room.

"Martin needs a mother, and I believe you are a good one. He also needs a father. Since I *am* his father, it seems the ideal solution is for us to marry. When I left Colorado, I thought that my son might be living in poverty. I intended to find him and make his life easier, but money doesn't seem to be any issue in his current situation. I've learned that your benefactor, John Boardman, left you well off, so it would be understood that we wouldn't be marrying for one another's money."

Rose lifted her hand. "Just a minute. Are you suggesting that a marriage between us would be a partnership just to benefit Martin? A legal arrangement?"

Edward cleared his throat, and he squirmed nervously.

"Well, I would expect it to be a marriage in the full meaning of the word. I would live here, or I could buy another house."

Rose stared at him with reproachful eyes. She swallowed hard, seething with anger and humiliation. Her curt voice lashed at him.

"Of all the arrogant men, you take the prize, Mr. Moody. You're forgetting one important person in this arrangement. Martin! He made it plain last week that he doesn't want anything to do with you, and he hasn't changed his mind. Until he does, I will not be a party to force him to do so."

Sallie entered with the well-filled tea tray, but Rose stopped her with a wave of her hand. She backed out of the room.

"As for marriage, Mr. Moody, if you think for a minute that I'd enter into a union such as you've described, you don't know much about women. I've prayed for years to find a man who loves me and whom I could love in return. I believe God will answer that prayer in His time. And when He does, I don't want to be tied up in a marriage of convenience."

Rose's voice faltered, and tears threatened to overflow, which only increased her anger. She didn't want to cry before this man who had hurt her so badly.

"I'm not for sale, and neither is my son. We are not interested in your proposition. Leave my house, and don't ever come back."

five

A few minutes later, Rose lay facedown on her bed, shoulders heaving, sobbing loudly, when Sallie found her. "Has he gone?" Rose asked.

"Yes, but he sent his apologies. Said he didn't mean to insult you. Whatever that means."

Rose rolled over on her back and sat, cross-legged, in the middle of the bed and wiped her eyes on the hem of her dress. She patted the bed beside her, and Sallie sat down. "Did you hear what he said to me?"

"Not much of it. I was in the kitchen fixin' the tea."

"He's made up his mind that if we get married, we could both have Martin. He could move in here, and we'd be one cozy, happy family."

"I figgered that was what he had in mind. He might have an eye on your money, too."

"Supposedly, he has plenty of money."

"But you ain't seen none of that coin, have you? Anything I've seen out of Mr. Moody so far ain't impressed me."

"I feel like taking Martin back to the *Vagabond* and asking Gramps to take off for parts unknown."

Sallie favored her mistress with a hearty laugh. "That don't sound much like the Rose Thurston I know—to give up without a fight."

A sheepish grin came over Rose's face. "I have a feeling I will have to fight, for I'm sure I haven't heard the last of Edward Moody." She slipped off the high bed and started unbuttoning her dress. She put on a plain gingham garment like the ones she had worn most of her life.

"I need to talk to Gramps and Granny. Ask Isaiah to go

to the school and walk home with Martin if I'm not back in time. I don't want him left unguarded at any time."

Rose tied a shawl around her shoulders, for the spring wind blowing off of the Ohio had a chill. She found Harry on the deck fishing, but he anchored his poles and went inside the shanty boat with Rose. Lottie sat in her chair piecing a quilt top.

"Hi, honey," she said. "What's troubling you?"

"Seems like I'm always coming to you with my troubles. But it's Edward Moody again." She explained in detail the things that had occurred with Edward in the past several days. "Do you think he can take Martin away from me?"

"Nah!" Harry said indignantly. "No court in Kentucky will allow that."

"If Mr. Moody has a lot of money, it could happen. I've known courts to be bought off before," Lottie countered sagely. "But I wouldn't worry, Rose. For one thing, Martin won't go with him, and God is on your side. You may have a lot of heartache before this is over, but right will win out."

"I've tried to tell myself that over and over, Granny, but I get down every once in a while, and I needed to talk to you about it. Do I smell gingerbread cookies?"

"Yeah," Lottie said, smiling. "I baked them this mornin'. I just had a feelin' you or Martin would stop by today."

Lottie lifted herself out of her rocker. She poured a cup of coffee and handed it to Rose. She sipped it gratefully. Harry always said that Lottie's coffee was stronger than a mule. Rose agreed, but today she needed a little extra power. She nibbled on one of the large cookies and drank the coffee and asked for more.

When she was ready to leave, Lottie gave her a plate of the cookies to take to Martin. "Sallie will have a fit for me sendin' vittles up there." She cackled. "But I like to bake cookies for my boy."

"I still wish you and Gramps would come live with me. You

could help Sallie with the cooking, and Gramps, you would be a help with Martin. I miss seeing you every day. Besides, he *does* need a man in his life."

"Now, honey," Lottie said. "We've been over this before. We'd be out of place in that fancy house. We've lived on the river too long to leave it now. Besides, we're going to spend the summer with you on the showboat, so that will be like old times."

Rose had known the answer before she asked, and she didn't blame her grandparents. She missed the river, too.

૨૪

Edward's anger soon dissipated, but he was still hurt by Rose's reaction. Why would marriage to him be such a terrible thing? Up until he had returned to Louisville, Edward had never considered marrying again, but he had plenty of women who had given him the opportunity. He must not be totally repulsive to women.

He and Martha had only been married a year when Martin was born. She had been ill during most of her pregnancy, so they had not been able to spend a lot of time getting to know each other, as most newlyweds do in creating a truly rewarding marriage. But once his craze for making a successful business life had been accomplished, he started realizing that he not only needed love but companionship, as well. During the few days he had contemplated proposing to Rose, he had actually started anticipating having a home.

When a few days passed and Rose hadn't contacted him, Edward's anger surfaced. He visited Duncan McKee again and asked him to start proceedings to gain custody of Martin. More than once he asked himself what he would do with the child if he did get him. He was an only child and had never lived in a house with another child. He supposed he could hire a nanny to raise the boy. But was that fair to Martin?

Edward conceded that he wasn't spiritually competent to raise the child and turned to God for wisdom.

God, I'm at my wit's end. I have no one else to turn to. What is the right thing to do?

Edward had packed a Bible when he started to Colorado, but in the hectic days he had spent in that state, he didn't know what had happened to it. At a retail store near the hotel, he bought a Bible. When he started reading it, Edward felt as if he were being reunited with an old friend.

As he found Bible passages that had been special to him when he was a youth, it was as if he were reading them for the first time. Many of the scriptures comforted Edward.

For I am persuaded, that neither death, nor life, nor angels, nor principalities, nor powers, nor things present, nor things to come, nor height, nor depth, nor any other creature, shall be able to separate us from the love of God, which is in Christ Jesus our Lord.

But other Bible passages condemned him—especially his lifestyle for so many years.

Lay not up for yourselves treasures upon earth. . .but lay up for yourselves treasures in heaven. . . . For where your treasure is, there will your heart be also.

He had failed to heed those words. He hadn't sent any treasures to heaven. All of his treasure had been stored in earthly banks. His father had left Edward financially sound. Why hadn't he been content to stay in Pittsburgh and carry on the foundry business that had prospered his father? Why had the lure of greater riches pulled him toward the West? He knew that Rose's accusation had been just. It was doubtful that Martha would have died if he hadn't been determined to invest in a get-rich-quick scheme.

Knowing it was too late to change the past, Edward prayed for God to give him the strength to make the right decisions now.

છે

When she didn't hear anything from Edward for several days, Rose began to breathe easier. She had finally mastered playing "Old Folks at Home" on the piano, and she and Martin enjoyed singing together. She had a strong soprano voice, and when Martin joined his childish tones to hers, the result was harmonious. They were in the parlor practicing on a new song when the doorknocker sounded. Rose's hands hovered momentarily over the keys as a strange sense of foreboding threatened her peace.

"I'll get it, Mama."

Martin ran to the front door, but he soon reappeared in the parlor door. "The man wouldn't give the letter to me. He said you had to sign for it."

With a sigh of resignation, Rose went to the door. The letter delivered by a deputy sheriff was from the office of Duncan McKee. She signed for the letter, thanked the deputy, and closed the door.

"What is it, Mama?" Martin asked.

If he hadn't been present when the message came, she would have tried to conceal it from him, but whatever it was, he should know. With her fingernail, she opened the seal and read aloud. "This is to notify you to be present in the court of Judge Roy Canterbury, Tuesday, April 20, for a hearing concerning the custody of Martin Moody. Plaintiff in the case, Edward Moody; the defendant, Rose Thurston."

She sat heavily on the sofa, and Martin leaned against her knees. "What does it mean, Mama? Is that man trying to take me away from you?"

She put her arm around him and drew him close. "Yes, that's what it means. But trying to do something and actually doing it are two different things. Don't worry about it. I'm glad he's doing this. If the judge decides in our favor, then we won't have any concern about him any longer."

"I'm afraid, Mama."

"Don't be. But let's go tell Granny and Gramps about this. They will need to know as soon as possible."

"Will Gramps go beat up on Mr. Moody?"

Despite the agony in her heart, Rose laughed at the

thought of wizened Harry Thurston doing physical battle with Edward Moody, who appeared as solid as the Rocky Mountains. "Of course not. Christians don't fight their battles that way. We're going to pray for God's will to be done."

"I would like to have a father, Mama, like the other boys, but I don't want Mr. Moody."

His comment saddened Rose. What could she have done to give her son a better attitude toward his father? She had tried everything possible to make him remember his parents with love. Could it be that her resentment of Edward Moody had come through to his son? And she knew she had resented Edward.

Did she still resent him? She wished she could be unconcerned about the man now. In the past week Rose had wondered if her anger at Edward's proposal stemmed from her own thoughts of marrying him to provide a family for Martin. But she didn't want it to be a business arrangement.

If she hadn't been so preoccupied with her own emotions, Rose would have noticed that Martin was quieter than usual during their visit with Harry and Lottie. But it came as a total surprise the next morning when Sallie went to Martin's room to get him ready for school and found an empty room. Martin hadn't slept in his bed.

Rose had just arisen when Sallie knocked and entered the room.

"Now I don't want to scare you, Miss Rose, but do you know where Martin is? Did he sleep in here last night?"

"What do you mean?"

"He's not in his room, and the bed is just like it was when I turned it down last night. Usually his bed looks like a tornado has struck when he gets up in the morning."

"I'll look for him as soon as I dress. He seemed extra quiet last night, and I knew he was worrying about this lawsuit. Maybe he slept in the barn, so he could be close to Tibbets."

"I'll send Isaiah to find out, and I'll be back in a minute to help you," Sallie said.

When Isaiah didn't find Martin in the barn, Rose rushed to the waterfront, praying that Martin had spent the night with her grandparents. Surely if he had gone to them in the middle of the night, Harry would have come to tell her. But she had to make sure.

Lottie saw Rose running down the riverbank, and she was on deck to meet her.

"Granny, is Martin here?"

"I ain't seen him since you left last night."

"He isn't at the house, and Sallie says he hasn't slept in his bed. I'm afraid he's run away."

"Maybe his father took him. The *Mary Ann* headed downriver this morning. Captain Parsons blew the whistle just as we got out of bed. Maybe Martin and his father were passengers."

Determined not to think the worst about Edward, she answered, "Martin wouldn't go with his father without a fuss. And I don't think Edward would take him without at least telling me. But I suppose I'd better check with him."

As worried as she was about Martin, Rose's steps lagged as she approached the hotel. What if Edward was gone? When she inquired about Edward, the clerk said, "He just came through the lobby from the dining room. He's up in his room."

"Was he alone?"

Looking at her strangely, the clerk said, "Yes, ma'am."

He looked at her even more strangely when she asked the number of Edward's room.

Rose ran up the stairs, really scared now. She pounded on Edward's door, and her tension was unbearable until she heard him unlatch the door.

"Why, Rose," he said, when she rushed past him and looked around the room.

"Do you have Martin?"

"No. What's wrong?" His voice was harsh with anxiety, and she knew he was telling the truth.

"He's gone! I think he's run away."

She told him quickly what had happened and where she had looked. "I didn't think you would steal him, but in a way, I hoped you had."

"What a thing to say!"

"But I knew you wouldn't harm him. I'm imagining all kinds of things."

Her shoulders slumped, and she started toward the door.

"Wait a minute until I put on my coat," he said, "and I'll go with you. Surely we can find him."

"Do you suppose he's been kidnapped?" Edward asked. "I'm sure there are people who know we each have money."

Rose shook her head. "I think he's run away. A bucket is gone from the kitchen, as well as some bread and cookies that Martin especially likes."

"Has he ever done anything like this before?"

"Never."

"Does he know about the lawsuit? Would he go to such lengths to keep from coming to me?"

"He was at the house when the notice came from Mr. McKee's office, and he was upset. Don't hold it against him, Edward. He's just a child. And he's been hurt. As he grows older, he'll be different."

She looked so helpless leaning against the doorjamb that Edward put his arm around her and hugged her slightly. "We'll find him. Do you have any idea where he might have gone?"

"I've already been to the *Vagabond*, and he isn't there," she murmured into the lapel of his coat. "You might go to the cemetery—he may have gone to his mother's grave, although he has never gone by himself. While you do that, I'll check on our showboat, the *Silver Queen*. He likes to play there sometimes."

"I'll meet you at the *Vagabond* after I've been to the cemetery." He released her. "Don't worry."

But no one had seen Martin around the waterfront, and when Edward came to the shanty an hour later, he hadn't found the child, either.

"Should I report his disappearance to the police, Gramps?" Rose asked.

"I'll do that," he said. "You go to school and find out if any of the kids know where he is."

Rose and Edward left the waterfront together and walked uptown. When they parted in front of Rose's house, Edward said, "It's all my fault. I'm sorry I came back, and even more sorry that I've caused you this trouble."

Now it was Rose's turn to comfort him, and she laid her hand on his arm. "Don't feel that way. I've been having my moments of self-incrimination, too—thinking that I've failed him, or he would have talked to me about how he felt. And Martin is at fault, too. I've taught him that Christians must forgive, and even a child can make the wrong decisions. He has always been hesitant to talk about the things that worry him."

With a wry grin, Edward said, "I'm afraid that's a trait he got from his father. It's probably best for me to leave the decisions up to you and your grandfather. I'll be at the hotel. Send for me if you need me."

But in spite of a thorough search of the city, the morning passed, and Martin wasn't found. Rose went to the *Vagabond* to be with her grandparents, for she knew they, too, were concerned about Martin. She ate supper with them, and after they washed the dishes, Lottie and Rose joined Harry on the deck where he was fishing. No matter what might be amiss, Harry kept busy.

Rose felt so helpless just sitting, waiting. But what else could she do? Volunteers were combing the town and the countryside looking for Martin. How could a ten-year-old boy have disappeared so completely?

A steamboat whistle sounded repeatedly downriver, and the three Thurstons exchanged puzzled glances. "That sounds like the *Mary Ann*," Harry said. "Cap Parsons just left out of here this morning, headin' for Cairo."

The familiar steamboat came into view, whistle sounding, black smoke pouring from the stack. Lottie shaded her eyes and peered into the gathering dusk. "It's the *Mary Ann* all right. What's the matter with Captain Parsons? He's got full steam on that boat and keeps blowing the whistle. Reckon he's got a sick man on board?"

With a quickening of her pulse, Rose had a happy thought, suspecting the reason for the captain's quick return. She hurried to the aft deck of the shanty when the *Mary Ann*'s speed slackened perceptibly, angling toward the *Vagabond*. Captain Parsons stood in the pilothouse, a small figure beside him.

"That's Martin," Rose said, and she waved her hand.

The *Mary Ann* drew to within a few yards of the shanty boat. Captain Parsons turned the wheel over to his mate and came out on the top deck, pulling the small boy.

"Hey!" he shouted. "I found a stowaway on my boat. Do you think I ought to throw him overboard?"

Laughing, Rose said, "If you do, be sure he lands on the deck of the shanty. I'm sorry he caused you so much trouble, Captain."

"I'll take some of Lottie's pies for my trouble next time I stop in Louisville."

"You've got yourself a deal, Captain!" Lottie shouted.

"And I'll even pitch in a mess of catfish," Harry added.

The giant paddlewheel slowed and lazily splashed a spray of water as it turned. One of the deckhands lowered a gangplank toward the deck of the *Vagabond*. Harry secured it. Head down, Martin plodded across the makeshift bridge. Lottie grabbed him and hugged him hard. Rose waved to the captain as he returned to the pilothouse, turned the *Mary Ann*, and headed downstream once again.

Peering from the safety of Lottie's arms, Martin asked, "Are you mad at me, Mama?"

"I've been too worried to get mad, son. But now that you're back safely, I probably will get mad. Why did you do such a thing?"

"I didn't want to leave you, Mama—I didn't want to go with Mr. Moody."

"You're too young to make decisions like that. Besides, when you hid on the *Mary Ann*, you were running away from *me*. How do you think that made me feel?" She discovered that her knees were trembling, either from relief or from anger. "Let's go home. Isaiah and Sallie will be worried. And I'll have to notify the police that you're safe."

"I'll take care of that," Harry said. "You look after the boy."

"Will you get word to Edward that Martin is all right, Gramps? He's very concerned, and he blames himself."

"Yes, I'll go to the hotel first."

❧

Edward hurried downstairs with a heavy heart when he was summoned by the front desk. Rose's grandfather was here to see him. If it was good news, he believed Rose would have come to tell him herself.

"Martin is all right," Harry hastened to tell him. "He hid away on Captain Parsons' boat, and the captain didn't find him until they were a far piece down the river. He turned around and brought the boy back. Rose took him home, but she wanted me to let you know."

"Thank you. I'm happy he's all right. I told Rose I was sorry, but I owe you and your wife an apology, too."

Harry negated his apology with a wave of his hand. "You were a boy yourself once, Mr. Moody. You know how notional a kid can be. I reckon most of us have run away at one time or another. I've got to tell the police now."

Remembering the time when he had run away from Martin, Edward returned to his room. What should he do?

He wanted to see Rose, but he wouldn't go to her house and further antagonize his son. Should he just forget about him and leave Louisville? But where would he go? He had sold his property in Colorado, so he had nothing to go back for. And after ten years away from Pittsburgh, he had no ties there.

He didn't want to leave the area. Even if he couldn't get custody of Martin he would like to see the child occasionally. But Edward needed to keep busy.

Edward decided to pass time by looking around Louisville for business investments. The river crest had come and gone, and the water was at its normal level. He often walked along the river in late evenings, experiencing a penetrating loneliness he had never known before.

One night he wandered toward the *Vagabond*. Martin sat on the deck with Harry, and they both had fishing lines in the water. Edward leaned against a tree, partly hidden by the foliage so they couldn't see him. It was obvious they enjoyed being together for he could hear them talking. Occasionally, he also heard Martin's childish laughter. So interested was he in the scene below him that he didn't hear Rose's approach.

&

Rose was walking to the *Vagabond* to pick up Martin after a visit with her grandparents, when she saw Edward watching Martin and Harry. She stopped in her tracks and watched him as intently as he was watching them. The sadness on his face dismayed her.

Perhaps sensing her presence, Edward turned quickly, starting guiltily that she had caught him spying. He turned away from her.

"Good evening, Edward," Rose said quietly, coming closer to him. "I came to walk home with Martin."

"Do you hate me, Rose?"

"No, of course not," she said, thinking that she liked him better now than she ever had. No longer was he the self-confident man she had known. The humility on his face brought tears to the surface of her eyes. She looked away, blinking, not wanting him to see her vulnerability to his presence.

She motioned to a wooden bench her grandfather had built in the shade of a tree. Lottie often came here to rest when the heat in the shanty was unbearable.

"Shall we sit down?"

He joined her on the bench. "I wouldn't blame you if you did hate me. I've caused you nothing but trouble. I should never have come back."

His self-deprecating attitude was more than she could handle, and she prayed for wisdom in dealing with him.

"Is Martin all right now?"

"He's not very happy with me," she said. "I've taken away several of his privileges. He's not allowed to ride his pony for two weeks. He goes to school and comes right home and then stays in the house. Tonight is the first time I've let him visit Gramps and Granny."

"I've decided to drop the custody suit," Edward interjected suddenly.

She looked at him in surprise. "Why?"

"What if I win? Martin hates me so much that he ran away at the thought of belonging to me. What would I do with the child? In the best interest of my son, I think I should leave. You were getting along fine until I showed up. Ten years ago I forfeited any right to call him my son."

Rose looked across the river, trying to find the right words. She longed for wisdom to know how to deal with the situation. "No. I want the judge to hear your side of the case. I'm not in a position to make an unbiased judgment. I'll make any sacrifice to do what's best for Martin. I will never voluntarily agree to give him up, but Judge Canterbury is not biased. He'll be fair. If he thinks you should have Martin, I'll accept it."

❧

Edward was shocked at Rose's words. He knew he would

never take the child away from Rose, no matter what the decision was. The more he was around her, the more he decided that his proposal to Rose was not as absurd as she had considered. He wasn't sure he was in love with Rose, yet, but given an opportunity, he believed he could become very fond of her. But after he had been rejected once, he felt that Rose would have to indicate that she was interested in his proposal before he spoke again. And as long as Martin refused to accept him, Rose wouldn't do anything to upset the boy.

"I'll be honest with you. Mr. McKee told me from the outset that he didn't think I had much of a case."

"We'll see," Rose said. "I'd better go get Martin," she added, rising to her feet. "He has a curfew to keep."

"How much longer will his punishment go on?" Edward asked, knowing that Rose was a good mother.

"Another week."

"I'd like to have dinner with you again, Rose."

She shook her head. "It isn't wise for you to fraternize with the enemy. Thanks for the invitation, though."

Edward watched the graceful movements of her body as she walked to the shanty boat. Sighing wistfully, he turned toward town. He found it difficult to think of Rose Thurston as an enemy.

six

Since it was a private hearing, only six people were in the courtroom when Judge Canterbury entered and took his seat behind the bench. Lottie and Harry had come with Rose and Martin. Edward and Duncan McKee sat at a desk on the opposite side of the aisle.

The judge read the papers on his desk; then he looked over his glasses at Rose. "You don't have an attorney, Miss Thurston?"

"No, Your Honor."

"Does that mean you are not contesting this claim?"

She stood, her knees shaking, a slight tremor in her voice. "Yes, I do contest it, but Martin's life with me is well-known to anyone who's interested in finding out. It's my opinion that I don't need any defense other than my record as a mother to Martin. However, if Your Honor has any questions, I believe I can answer them satisfactorily."

Judge Canterbury nodded.

"Mr. McKee, you represent the plaintiff in this case?"

Mr. McKee stood. "Yes, Your Honor. Edward Moody is the father of the child known as Martin Moody Thurston."

The judge raised his hand. "Just a minute." He turned to Rose. "Do you agree to that?"

"Yes, Your Honor. I saw Mr. Moody the night Martin was born on the *Vagabond*. I recognized him as soon as he returned to Louisville."

"Go ahead, Mr. McKee."

"Your Honor, Mr. Moody is suing to have the adoption of his son by Rose Thurston overturned. Since he didn't give his approval to this adoption, he contends that the action is illegal."

Martin scooted closer to Rose, and she put her arm around him.

"Is your client bringing any charges of neglect against the defendant?"

"No, Your Honor. He simply wants to be acknowledged as the child's father and rightful guardian. We've submitted a folder of Mr. Moody's assets to prove that he is able to provide for his son."

"I've already deliberated several hours about this case. But before I give my judgment, I want to hear from the one most affected by my decision. Martin Moody Thurston, will you stand, please?"

Martin cringed even closer to Rose. She smiled and encouraged him to stand. He looked small and vulnerable, but he stood straight, a determined look on his face.

"Martin," the judge inquired, "are you aware of what these proceedings mean? If I decide in favor of Mr. Moody, he will assume the role of your father. If I decide against Mr. Moody's appeal, you will continue to live with your mother as you've been doing. Do you understand?"

Martin nodded, whispering, "Yes, sir."

"I will make a decision based on what I feel is best for everyone, but I think it's only fair to give you the opportunity to make your wishes known. What is your opinion?"

God, Rose prayed, *don't let him say anything to hurt Edward. I know what my son wants, but I don't want him to embarrass his father.*

In a barely audible voice, Martin said, "Mr. Moody may be a very nice man, but I don't know him. He's a stranger to me. But I love my mama—I want to stay with her."

"Thank you, Martin," the judge said. "You may sit down."

Sniffing, Martin sat close to Rose, and she smoothed his hair and caressed his shoulders.

"All of you may stay seated while I state my decision. Mr. Moody," he said, "I'm a father myself, and I can sympathize with your desire to have your son. I don't doubt that, somewhere in the multitude of adoption cases on the books in this country, there's a law that would substantiate your claim. But here in Kentucky, we're a little behind the big courts in the eastern cities. I don't know any such law, and I'm not going to look for one."

He paused, and the silence in the room was breathtaking.

"I was the judge of this court and made the decision for Miss Thurston to adopt this boy. At that time, she indicated that you had been gone for three years, and that she had no knowledge of whether you were dead or alive. She also testified that you had given the child to her. Is that correct?"

Shamefaced, Edward said, "Yes, Your Honor."

The judge nodded. "I've watched your son grow strong, and he's been happy under Miss Thurston's care. Her character is above reproach. She has the financial means to provide for the boy. And I personally feel that it would be a travesty of justice to annul Martin's adoption. So I'm deciding against you, Mr. Moody. It is possible that if you appeal to a higher court, you may receive a different decision."

"Mama, does that mean I can stay with you?" Martin asked with excitement.

Rose put a finger to her lips to silence him, but she nodded slightly. Martin's mouth spread into a wide grin.

Mr. McKee stood. "Your Honor, I will discuss an appeal with my client, but in the meantime, could he be awarded visiting privileges with his son?"

"Mr. McKee, the defendant has legal custody of the child. It's up to Martin and Miss Thurston to decide if your client has any contact with the boy. It will violate the order of this court if your client forces a relationship with the child."

Edward touched Mr. McKee's arm. "I will not appeal this decision," he said quietly.

"Your Honor, Mr. Moody has indicated that he will not continue his suit farther."

"Very well," Judge Canterbury said. He pounded his desk with a gavel. "This court is adjourned."

The judge stepped down from the bench and shook hands with Rose and her parents. He patted Martin's head.

"Thank you, Judge Canterbury," Rose said. When the judge left the room, Martin laughed happily and hugged Harry and Lottie. Rose found it difficult to join in their merrymaking when she saw Edward leaving the courtroom alone. She felt sorry for him, for she knew the agony she had experienced in the past few weeks when she thought there was a possibility she would lose her son. If Martin weren't so biased against his father, would she accept Edward's proposal of marriage?

The next morning, Edward sent a message asking Rose to have dinner with him that night at the hotel. Knowing that matters had not been settled between Edward and her, Rose didn't hesitate to accept the invitation.

&

Rose found Edward waiting for her in the lobby. "Thanks for coming," he said. "I wouldn't have blamed you if you had refused."

He took her arm and escorted her into the dining room, and he asked for a secluded table. They spoke of trivialities while the waiter brought their beverages. Edward's eyes seemed desolate, and Rose missed the self-confidence always so evident in his speech and manner.

"I wanted to see you once more before I left town. I thought it was wiser not to come to your home."

Rose sensed an immediate pang of disappointment, and her voice broke slightly when she replied, "You're leaving? So soon?"

"There isn't any reason for me to stay. It will make things easier for you and Martin if I'm not here."

Rose wasn't prepared for the sense of loss she experienced, knowing that she wouldn't see Edward again. She wasn't sure she was successful in concealing her consternation from him.

"Where are you going?"

He shook his head. "I don't have any close relatives in Pittsburgh, except my wife's sister and her family. And I sold out my businesses in Colorado. I haven't decided yet where I will go. Maybe to California."

Choosing her words carefully, Rose said, "Then why don't you stay in Louisville a little longer. I still have much to learn about children, but I know that they change their minds often. Given time, I believe Martin will soften toward you. Did you notice at the trial he didn't say he hated you, but that you were a stranger to him?"

"I don't want to leave," Edward admitted, "but I don't want my presence to be an embarrassment to you."

"And I appreciate that. My conscience hurts because you were denied the right to see Martin. If he ever decides to pursue a relationship with you, I won't oppose it."

"Then you don't mind if I stay?"

She reached her left hand across the table, and Edward clasped it tightly. "I don't mind at all," she said.

Edward leaned forward and kissed her fingertips. "Then I will stay for the time being."

The waiter came with their food, and Edward released her hand reluctantly. "I also had another reason for seeing you tonight. I was in the lobby this morning when a man arrived from New York. He introduced himself to the clerk as Walt Boardman and stated that he had come to settle the estate of his uncle, John Boardman. Isn't that your benefactor?"

"Why, yes," Rose said, surprised. "I was the only beneficiary in John's will. I didn't know he had any close relatives. He lived here for years and didn't mention any family at all. I suppose everyone assumed he didn't have anyone."

"Could this man cause you any trouble?"

"I hardly think so," Rose said slowly. "It's been over a year since John died. The showboat was in dock all last summer because the estate wasn't settled. The will has been probated, and it's on record in the courthouse. But if John did have relatives and didn't mention them in the will, could that cause a problem? I've heard that close relatives can make a claim unless they are given at least a dollar."

"I don't know anything about Kentucky laws, but if Boardman was in sound mind and body when he made his will, it won't be easy to break."

"He had made the will two years prior to his death," Rose said.

"You might want to discuss the matter with an attorney."

Rose nodded. "I'll do that."

"May I walk you home?"

"No, thank you. Isaiah should be waiting with the phaeton."

❧

When Rose arrived home from church the next day, a carriage was drawn up in front of the house, and a man sat on the porch. He wore impeccable clothing, and Rose suspected immediately who he was. In fact, he had the same large head and piercing black eyes that had characterized John Boardman's appearance.

He stood when she and Martin approached the house.

"Are you Miss Thurston?"

She nodded.

"Then let me introduce myself. I'm Walter Boardman. I've come to town to settle my uncle's affairs. My father is his closest relative, but he was unable to travel so far. As I understand, you've been looking after the house since my uncle's death. I've brought my trunk from the hotel—if you'll call one of the servants to haul it inside."

Convinced that the man knew the state of affairs exactly, she immediately mistrusted his amiable attitude.

"I beg your pardon, Mr. Boardman, but I'm not 'taking care of the place.' It belongs to me. John willed his whole estate to me, and the proper legal procedures have been concluded. I have two helpers only, and they already have all the work they can do. We're not equipped to take in overnight guests."

"You're making a big mistake, ma'am. My father bankrolled John when he moved to Kentucky, and he never paid back a red cent. It won't take long for me to prove that the property is mine. I might as well look the place over."

"No," Rose said, wishing Harry or Isaiah was here.

As if in answer to her wish, Isaiah strolled around the corner of the house. Having just returned from church, he was dressed in his Sunday clothes. He flashed a belligerent glance toward Boardman. "Do you need somethin', Miss Rose?"

Glancing at Isaiah, Boardman said, "Is this your man? He can carry in my trunk."

Shaking her head at Isaiah, Rose said, "He is *not* my man. He works here as he did for John before me. And I told you that I'm not equipped for overnight guests."

Favoring Rose with a withering gaze, he said, "Very well. I'll leave, but I'll be back."

"As a matter of curiosity, why have you waited so long? John died over a year ago."

"We only recently learned of his death." He spat out the words angrily. Rose felt suddenly weak and scared in the face of his anger. She sank weakly into a white wooden chair on the porch as he stalked toward his carriage.

Martin, who had been a silent spectator to the whole episode, said, "Does that mean we can move back to the *Vagabond*, Mama?"

Rose laughed and ruffled his fair head. Her efforts to turn him into a gentleman weren't progressing much better than her attempts to become a lady. But it pleased Rose that he hadn't lost the down-to-earth values that she had taught him.

From the bottom of the steps, Isaiah stared after Boardman. "Who is that, Miss Rose?"

"John Boardman's nephew. He came prepared to move in here and prove that his father was John's heir."

"Can he do it?"

"He can try, I suppose. I know John thought he was doing me a favor by making me an heiress. But I don't know why anybody wants to be rich. If you're poor, nobody is trying to take anything away from you. I've just proved my right to have Martin, and now it looks as if I'll have to get a lawyer to prove John's will is valid. I can't wait to get on the *Silver Queen* and leave Louisville for a few months."

❧

Even though Rose had appeared unconcerned about Walter Boardman, Edward had dealt with men of his caliber many times, and he made it a point to watch the man.

Monday evening when he went for dinner in the hotel's dining room, Edward tipped the waiter to give him a table close to Boardman, who was having dinner with three other men. Edward hadn't seen them before, but the men were burly, uncouth characters whom he immediately mistrusted. While ostensibly interested only in his food, Edward took in every word from the nearby table. He was furious when he learned that Boardman had hired these men to go with him to Rose's house in the middle of the night and evict her. With an effort, he controlled his temper.

Moving leisurely so Boardman wouldn't suspect that his plans had been overheard, Edward ate most of the food on his plate. But as soon as he returned to the lobby, he rushed upstairs to his room and put a gun in his pocket. To protect Rose and her household, he needed the advice of someone older and wiser than he was. He borrowed a lantern from the hotel clerk and hurried toward the waterfront. He figured the Thurstons would already be in bed, but Harry was still on the deck, setting trotlines for his nightly catch of fish.

"Mr. Thurston," he called from the bank. "It's Edward Moody. There's an emergency, and I must talk to you. May I come aboard?"

"Yeah, son. Watch your step on that plank. It gets slippery when the dew settles at night."

Edward held the lantern so Harry could see his face as he crossed the narrow board. "Rose has told you, I suppose, about John Boardman's nephew being in town."

"Yep. Sounds like he's gonna make trouble for my girl."

Edward nodded his head. "And right away, too. I sat close to Boardman in the restaurant tonight. He's hired some men, and they're intending to break into Rose's house tonight and put her out."

"Are they now?" Harry said, hitching up his pants, his nostrils twitching like a warhorse heading into battle. "That's easier said than done."

"Will you go to Rose's house and tell her, while I try to round up some help? We'll give Boardman a warm reception when he gets there."

Harry scratched his head. "Just a minute. I've got a better idea. You don't know people here like I do. I'll rouse Lottie out of bed, and the two of you can go warn Rose. I'll pick up two or three men who know how to fight, and we'll be there right away. Do you know what time they're planning to attack?"

"He didn't say exactly, but I'd judge it will be after the town settles for the night. Probably after midnight."

"That will give us plenty of time to get ready," Harry said as he disappeared inside the shanty, calling, "Lottie, get up—we've got trouble."

Ten minutes later, Lottie and Edward headed uptown toward Rose's home.

"You've done your part now, Mr. Moody," Lottie said, "by warning us. Don't feel you have to make any more trouble for yourself."

"It isn't any trouble, Mrs. Thurston. Besides, the attack may come before Harry gets there with his men. I might be needed."

"We may need your help—that's a fact. Rose's handyman, Isaiah Taylor, will be good if it comes to a fight. The two of you can hold them off until Harry comes."

Edward was relieved that the Thurstons had accepted his help so readily. The thought of Rose and Martin being in danger distressed him, and he wanted to do all he could to keep them safe.

"Rose and Martin sleep upstairs, and they might be hard to rouse," Lottie said. "Isaiah and Sallie live in a one-story house in the back, and they'll have a key to the mansion. We'll wake them, and Sallie can let us in the big house."

Edward was relieved when they reached Third Street and saw that Rose's house was dark. They had arrived in time.

Lottie motioned him around to the back, and she stopped at the door of a small cottage. She knocked twice, then said, "Don't shoot, Isaiah. It's me, Lottie." She chuckled quietly. "Isaiah sleeps with a shotgun under the bed. Didn't want to take no chances."

Edward heard footsteps approaching the door. "Who is it?" Isaiah said in his deep voice.

"It's Lottie, Rose's grandma. Mr. Moody is with me." Isaiah opened the door. "What's goin' on to bring you out this late of a night?" he asked.

"Let us come in and close the door," Lottie said. Sallie entered the living room, wrapped in a long robe, carrying a lighted lamp. Nodding toward Edward, Lottie said, "Mr. Moody overheard that Boardman feller planning to break in on Rose tonight and kick her out of the house."

Sallie put her hand over her mouth to stifle a scream. She set the lamp on a table and turned the flame low.

"Don't surprise me," Isaiah said, his black eyes gleaming angrily. "Meanest acting man I've seen in many a day."

"Can you let us inside the house to warn Rose and Martin?" Edward said. "Harry is bringing more men. We're planning a surprise for Mr. Boardman and his friends."

"Count me in on that welcome party," Isaiah said. "Let me get my gun."

"I hope they don't come until Harry gets here so he can

tell us what to do," Edward said. "But I doubt we will have to shoot anybody."

"A little buckshot aimed in the right direction might scare them away."

"I've got a gun in my pocket, too, if we need it," Edward admitted, "but I'm hoping they'll run when they find out they aren't dealing with only a woman and a child. But Harry will tell us what to do when he gets here. Right now, Sallie, you and Lottie should warn Rose. I'll go inside the house and be on guard there, Isaiah, if you'll watch from the yard."

Sallie stepped into a pair of shoes and lifted a large key off a hook beside the door.

"Isaiah, blow out that lamp," she said. "We can see to get to the house with the light from Mr. Moody's lantern. It's better if we don't have any lights—make 'em think we're all asleep."

The last few days Edward had fretted about Rose and Martin living alone, but after seeing the loyalty and efficiency of Sallie and Isaiah, his fears lessened. He walked behind Sallie and Lottie, carrying the lantern so that it lighted their path. The scent of spring flowers stung his nostrils, and he wondered why evil should be afoot on such a beautiful night. A night like this was meant for love and praise to God, not violence.

They entered the house through the kitchen, and Lottie plodded quietly toward the central hall. "Sallie, you go tell Martin," she said, "and I'll get Rose up."

⋙

Rose always slept with her door open in case Martin called her during the night, and she kept a lamp burning in the upper hallway. She roused quickly when she heard voices murmuring in the central hall downstairs. She recognized Sallie's voice, which didn't startle her, thinking the house-keeper had forgotten some task that needed to be done.

When she identified Lottie's voice, she *was* disturbed. She got out of bed, pulled on her robe, and rushed into the hallway. She picked up the lamp and started downstairs.

Halfway down, she paused, saying, "Granny, what's wrong? Has something happened to Gramps?"

Lottie moved up the steps toward her. "No, honey—nothing like that, but there is some trouble."

Sallie passed them on the steps. "I'm gonna wake Martin."

"What *is* wrong?" Rose demanded.

"Boardman is planning to kick you out of the house tonight and move in himself." Pointing over her shoulder, she said, "Mr. Moody heard him planning the attack and came to warn us."

Rose lifted her head and looked toward the lower hall. She hadn't realized anyone had come with Rose and Sallie. Her eyes connected with Edward's, and she was speechless.

Rose had been thinking about Edward when she had gone to bed, and it seemed that he had stepped out of her dreams. She flushed when she looked at her grandmother and saw the smug expression on Lottie's face as she glanced from Rose to Edward.

☙

From the first day he had seen her, Edward had wanted to see Rose's hair hanging around her shoulders. The lamp she held illuminated her face, which was framed with her golden hair. She wore a white, long-sleeved, floor-length robe over her nightgown.

He had once seen a painting of an angel descending from heaven on a gilded stairway. Rose could have posed for that artist. Her disheveled hair hung halfway to her waist. Her face was shadowed, and he couldn't make out the expression in her eyes. If he hadn't felt anything special for Rose before, Edward knew at this moment that he was beginning to care deeply for her. He refused to consider the barriers preventing any mutual happiness for them. Tonight he was only thankful that God had given him this opportunity to protect her—a task he would like to take on for a lifetime.

seven

The special moment Rose felt between Edward and her was shattered when Martin ran down the hallway. "Mama," he shouted excitedly, "Sallie says there's going to be a fight. Really?"

"I don't know. Mr. Moody brought the word. Let's see what he can tell us."

Martin looked down and saw Edward. "Oh, him!" he said disgustedly and slumped down on the stairs.

Rose saw pain spread across Edward's face, and a sharp reprimand hovered on her tongue. But she stifled it and left the boy to Sallie. She went downstairs and stopped beside Edward and gave him her hand. "Thank you. Will you tell me what you know?"

He explained what he had overheard and that he had gone to Harry for advice. "He's bringing some men to help scare Boardman and his men away. He sent your grandmother and me to warn you. Hopefully, he'll get here before Boardman arrives, but Isaiah is on guard outdoors. I think the two of us can keep them out of the house until Harry gets here."

Sallie now stood on the bottom step. "I ain't too bad in a fight, either, Mr. Moody."

"I'll go upstairs and dress," Rose said, "and I'll be right down." She patted the dejected Martin on the head as she passed him, but that was all the time she had for him now. They had to get ready for what was coming.

❧

Edward watched as, working by candlelight, Sallie prepared some coffee. It was ready when Harry arrived with three wiry-looking men, who appeared as if they would be able to take care of themselves in a fight.

"All was quiet on the street when we passed through town," Harry reported.

"I hope I haven't gotten you out on a wild goose chase," Edward said. "But I'm sure Boardman said he would strike tonight."

Rose had changed her robe and nightgown for a plain dress when she came downstairs. She had thrust a couple of combs in her hair to hold it away from her face, but it still fell from the crown of her head like a waterfall.

Martin had sneaked down the stairs, and he sat sullenly on the bottom step.

Ignoring him, Edward asked, "Harry, what plans do you have? Give us some orders."

Harry shook his head. "You're more a man of the world than I am, Mr. Moody. Since you've been in Colorado for years, you've probably seen your share of fighting. You take charge."

Without argument, Edward said, "Don't do any shooting unless we have to. We can't take the chance of killing someone and get into trouble with the law. However, it will be all right for Isaiah to shoot his shotgun in the air to scare them." He parted the curtains in the parlor and peered toward the silent street.

"There are six of us men. Four of us will go outside to intercept the would-be intruders and hopefully drive them away before they get inside the house. Two of you will stay inside, in case they break through our lines."

"You say not to shoot, mister," one of Harry's friends said, "but this ain't goin' be no picnic. Can we rough 'em up some?"

"We may have to for self-protection. And we have the right to do that. I can't give you a lot of orders when I don't know what to expect. Just use your best judgment."

He walked into the parlor and looked out the front window. "I'll go outside," he said. But glancing toward the women, he added, "Maybe you'd better stay here, Harry. Do you have any better suggestions?"

"No," Harry said, apparently content with Edward's handling of the situation.

"All right. Choose the men to go with me. Put out all of the lights so Boardman will think Rose and Martin are sleeping. Once your eyes are adjusted to the darkness, you can probably feel your way around. I'd suggest that the women and Martin go upstairs."

"No," Rose objected immediately. "This is my property they're trying to take."

Lottie and Sallie also stated their refusal to hide in the bedrooms. Edward glanced at Martin, who looked like he was glued to the first stair. He had his chin cupped in his hands and his elbows on his knees. His stubborn expression reminded Edward of himself and smiling, his eyes met Rose's.

"I'll watch him," she said softly.

Harry named off the men who would go with Edward. "Let's take time to pray," he said, and he knelt stiffly on the floor.

Surprised at himself, Edward soon found himself on his knees beside Harry.

"Lord God, You protected Daniel in the lions' den. You looked out for Joseph in Egypt. You led Moses across a tolerable stretch of desert. We believe You've got the same power today, and that You can reach out and touch us tonight. This trouble ain't of our own makin'. We're holdin' You to Your promise from the book of Psalms—'Let all those that put their trust in thee rejoice: let them ever shout for joy, because thou defendest them.' We're praisin' You tonight, God, and lookin' to You for deliverance. And all God's people said, amen."

Edward found himself joining the chorus of amens shouted around him, and it felt good. Yes, it felt good to be praising God after so many years. He had sensed that Rose had knelt beside him, and he turned toward her and took her hand to help her to her feet.

"Be careful," she whispered.

Edward stationed Isaiah and one of the men in the backyard, in case the attackers came that way. There was no covered porch on Rose's house, just a narrow area with a few chairs. He sat in a chair, hidden by a blooming bush. His companion knelt on the ground a few yards away. The gas-burning streetlight dimly illuminated the front lawn where a piece of marble statuary gleamed in the faint light.

A clock in the belfry of a nearby church struck the midnight hour, and Edward started worrying. Had he been mistaken in what Boardman planned to do? Had he reacted too quickly because of his concern for Rose? He had heaped all kinds of incrimination on himself when his companion cleared his throat in warning.

A lone man walked up the street. He paused before the house, looked around carefully, walked into the yard, and circled the house. Edward and his companion sat as statues, and apparently Isaiah and his buddy also stayed hidden. After a few minutes the man reappeared. He hurried to the street, whistled, and gave a beckoning summons with his arm.

The *clip-clop* of a horse's hooves sounded in the quietness of the night. Edward hunkered down beside the man hidden in the bush. "What do you make of it?" he asked.

"They're bein' cagey. That man wanted to be sure no one was on guard before the whole gang came. The fellers in the back must have stayed out of sight, too."

"That's the way I figured it," Edward said. "That wasn't Boardman. I want to catch him in the act."

Edward crawled across the porch and knelt behind another shrub. He spread the branches to give him a view of the street. A wagon drew up. Two men sat on the seat, and the wagon was filled with two trunks and several satchels. Another man sat in the wagon bed, so that meant they had at least four men to deal with. Edward recognized Boardman by the black Homburg hat he was wearing.

Anger surged through Edward. How dare this man plan an attack on Rose and her son! He always thought of Martin as *her* child now. He knew it was only fair that he would have to patiently earn the right to call the boy *his* son.

The four men walked in a close-knit group on the paving stones until they almost reached the porch. Boardman gestured with his arms, and two of the men started around opposite sides of the house. After waiting a minute or two, Boardman approached the house. When he put his feet on the first step, Edward rose from his hiding place.

"A little late for a social call, isn't it?" he said.

Boardman gasped and stepped backward.

"Who are you? What are you doing here?" he demanded.

"I might ask you the same thing. But to ease your mind, I'll tell you I'm Edward Moody. I'm a guest in the hotel where you're staying. I overheard your scheme to put Miss Thurston out of her home, and I decided to deal myself a hand in the game."

Looking wildly around him, Boardman said to his companion, "Rush him!"

When the rogue started toward Edward, Harry's friend, hidden by the bush, jumped up, turned the man around, and slugged him. He crumpled in a heap on the grass.

Apparently enraged over his thwarted plans, Boardman stepped close to Edward and planted a solid fist on his jaw. The move surprised Edward, and he staggered backward. When Boardman tried to take advantage of his successful punch, Edward was ready for him. He hit Boardman on the chin with a powerful whack that lifted him off his feet. Edward followed up his advantage with another blow to the stomach that immobilized Boardman, who spread-eagled at the foot of the steps.

In the silence that followed, Edward heard the blast of Isaiah's shotgun. He quickly tied the hands of Boardman's accomplice and motioned for his companion to watch Board-man. Within two minutes the other two attackers walked around the house with their hands lifted over their heads. Isaiah plodded behind them, holding his shotgun menacingly. His companion carried a lighted lantern.

"Harry!" Edward shouted. "Come on out. We've got things under control."

Harry still held his rifle when he stepped out on the porch, and he, too, brought a lantern. Rose came behind him, with Martin clutching her robe.

"What are we going to do with them?" Edward asked.

"Send for the police to haul 'em off to jail," Harry said. "They'll probably try to lie their way out of it, and say we attacked them, but they didn't have no business on this property."

"You take care of that, and the rest of us will guard them until the police get here."

"Isaiah, how about hitchin' up the phaeton to drive me to the central station? I hope Lieutenant Bell is on duty."

"Yes, sir, Mr. Harry. Back in a minute."

The other man, who had been guarding inside the house, stepped out on the narrow porch. He took Isaiah's shotgun and held it ready.

When Edward turned his head, Rose touched his cheek. "You're hurt," she said anxiously.

"Not much," Edward said, rubbing his burning jaw. He was embarrassed that he was the only one of the men who had a wound of any kind. "I didn't dodge in time, and Boardman hit me."

"Come inside. Sallie has some liniment that will help."

"Maybe after the police come. I'm all right now."

"Thank you," she said softly, so softly, he wasn't sure anyone else heard. She reached for his hand and squeezed it gently.

❧

Edward's gaze held to Rose's for a long moment, sending a

private message, but conscious of Martin trembling beside her, Rose turned away.

"Come inside, Martin. Mr. Moody and Gramps's friends will keep watch. We'll be safe now."

They found Lottie and Sallie in the kitchen. Lottie was stirring the coals in the stove and adding fuel for a quick blaze.

"We're fixin' some coffee for the men, Miss Rose."

"I'm sure they will like that," Rose agreed, her voice shaking. "I could use a cup myself."

Lottie was spreading thick slices of bread with butter and jam. She looked at Martin's frightened face and said, "Come help me, Martin."

"Wash your hands first," Rose said.

Now that Martin was occupied, Rose returned to the porch. Boardman had regained consciousness, but he was still lying on the ground. When he saw her, he snarled, "You're going to be in big trouble having these rowdies beat me up."

He started swearing at her, and Edward hopped off the porch and planted one of his feet on Boardman's stomach.

"Stop it," he said, applying pressure to Boardman's midsection. "You got what you deserved—sneaking in here in the middle of the night expecting to find a woman and a child alone."

"This house is mine," Boardman said.

"If you can prove you have a legal right to Boardman's estate, I'm sure Miss Thurston will move out. But you know that you have no claim to it. And I'll personally see that you don't steal it from her."

"She won't get away with this," Boardman said unrepentantly. "She's in trouble."

"I told you I'm the one who's responsible for upsetting your plans, Boardman. If you want to blame anyone, I'm the one."

"I don't know why you'd champion her. Way I hear it, she stole your boy just like she stole Uncle John's. . ."

Again Edward applied some pressure to Boardman's abdomen, cutting off his words.

"Then you heard wrong. I gave my boy to her ten years ago."

Rose realized that Martin and Lottie had joined them on the porch with a tray of sandwiches. No doubt Martin had heard everything. Would this admission make him hate his father even more?

A paddy wagon soon arrived, with Isaiah and Harry following in the phaeton. Lieutenant Bell and his deputy handcuffed the four men. While his deputy took them to the wagon, the lieutenant, whom Rose had known all of her life, said, "I'll hold them overnight, Rose, but I don't know how much of a case I can build against them. Because you were forewarned, and they didn't have the opportunity to do any damage, I don't know exactly what I can charge them with—probably no more than trespassing."

"Do what you can," she answered.

After the police left, Rose asked everyone to come inside for some coffee.

"If you can make a bed for Lottie and me," Harry said, "we'll spend the rest of the night here."

"Of course, you can stay. You can sleep in that small bedroom across from the kitchen where John slept most of the time."

"I'll fix the bed, Miss Rose," Sallie said.

"I'll do that while you and Granny serve some food to our helpers." When the others turned toward the dining room, Rose said, "Do you want to help me, Martin? Let's go upstairs and get some sheets and pillowcases. And you can bring a quilt from the linen closet."

❧

Edward watched Rose and Martin climb the stairs, but before he went to the dining room, he drew Harry aside.

"Boardman doesn't strike me as the kind of man to give up easily. Don't tell Rose about this, but if you can find a couple of men who'll guard the house at night, I'll pay them."

Looking keenly at him, Harry nodded. "I had the same notion. I think Lottie and me will have to move in for a spell. At least till Boardman leaves town or until Rose takes the showboat out in a few weeks. 'Course if Boardman is still around, there will have to be a guard posted during that time, too. But you won't have to pay for it—Rose has lots of money."

"I want to help," Edward insisted. "For the time being I intend to stay in Louisville. You take any steps you think are necessary to protect Rose and her property, and I'll help foot the bill."

Harry favored Edward with a sly grin, as if he would like to comment on Edward's attitude, but he only said, "I'll keep in touch with you. You gonna be at the hotel?"

"I'm not sure. I've been talking to Mr. Duncan about buying some property in Louisville. I'll let you know if I move."

Edward had no intention of leaving Louisville as long as there was an opportunity to pursue a closer relationship with Rose. Their future depended on Martin, and he wanted to be reconciled to his son, too. He had to win the boy's confidence before he could approach Rose, and that would take time. But Edward was a worker, and he had to have something to do while he bided his time to repair the breach with his son.

ও

Since Edward knew Rose wanted him to stay in Louisville, he started looking for a place to live. He had soon grown weary of the hotel's restaurant, and he ate most of his meals at the Kentucky Diner, a large eating place near the waterfront.

He had noticed a FOR SALE sign in the window of the diner on his first visit. When he asked questions, he learned that the owner had died and that his daughter, who lived in another state, wanted to sell the restaurant, lock, stock, and barrel, which included a furnished apartment on the second floor.

Edward looked over the restaurant's books and decided that the business was a good investment. He had owned a restaurant in Colorado, but he hadn't been directly responsible for operating it. A man had owed him money he couldn't pay, and when the man skipped out without paying his debt, Edward took over the business.

He approached Duncan McKee to help with the purchase, which was completed quickly, because Edward had already transferred some of his assets to the First National Bank of Louisville. Since he had no knowledge about operating a restaurant, he chose to put a great deal of the responsibility in the hands of the employees who had worked for the former owner.

The three-room apartment was adequate for his personal lodging for the time being. Edward asked Lottie to suggest a housekeeper for him, and he hired Mrs. McClary, a staid Irish woman, who came in three days a week to see to his needs.

Boardman and his three hired men had stayed in jail overnight, paid their fine, and been released. He had not left town as Edward had hoped, and he was convinced that Boardman wouldn't easily give up his scheme to take Rose's property.

ᐟᐟ

One night when she couldn't sleep, Rose peered out her bedroom window to look at the stars. Her heart skipped a beat when she noticed a man standing in the shadows along the street. Frightened, she woke Harry, who explained that the man was part of the protection Edward had insisted on providing. He also told her that at Edward's expense, he had hired a man to stay on the *Vagabond* at night to keep it from being destroyed while he and Lottie lived in Rose's house. Two of the men who had helped forestall Boardman's takeover of Rose's home alternated guarding her home during the night hours.

This information pleased Rose, who was a bit annoyed at

Edward, whom she hadn't seen since the night he had come to her rescue. The court order had stipulated that Edward wasn't to seek Martin's company without Rose's permission, and apparently Edward didn't intend to force his company upon them. She had learned that he had bought the restaurant and settled in town. She decided to talk to Martin about seeing his father.

On Saturday afternoon, Rose had Isaiah saddle her mare and Martin's pony, and they rode out to the cemetery. After they had pulled the weeds from his mother's burial plot, they walked to the point where they could see Louisville's harbor.

"Martin," Rose began, "I know you don't like Mr. Moody, and I can understand why you feel hard toward him. However, I *do* like him. He's been very fair about your adoption, and certainly he was a big help when Walt Boardman tried to drive us from our home. As a thank-you gesture, I want to invite him to dinner some evening. I'm not forcing you to talk to Mr. Moody. And you won't have to eat with us—you can eat with Isaiah and Sallie. However, I won't invite him if you object."

"Will Grandpa and Granny eat with you?"

"Gramps likes Mr. Moody and provides fish for his restaurant. Granny appreciates what he did for us. I'm certain they'll be glad to entertain him."

"And you won't invite him if I say no?"

"That's right. I'm leaving the decision up to you," Rose said. She crossed the fingers of her mind, thinking, *at least for the time being.* Edward was constantly in her mind, and she knew she couldn't deny her heart much longer. Hopefully, she could have her heart's desire with Martin's blessing, but she had to move slowly.

"Well, I guess it's all right. But I want to eat in the kitchen with Sallie and Isaiah."

Thank God from whom all blessings flow, Rose thought, joy flooding her heart. But she retained a nonchalant attitude with Martin.

"Then I'll send an invitation to him."

They were almost back to the horses when Martin said, "He sure took care of those mean men, didn't he?"

"Yes."

"Will he feel bad if I don't eat with you?"

"Why, I don't think so. He understands why you don't like him."

"Oh," Martin said, and he remained thoughtful and silent during the rest of their ride.

❧

With trembling fingers and many false starts, Rose composed the invitation without giving much information. She didn't know how much Edward would read between the lines.

> *Dear Edward:*
> *Will you come for supper tomorrow evening, six o'clock? Granny, Gramps, and I will look forward to your company. Although Martin approved the invitation, he's chosen to eat in the kitchen. Don't be hurt by that. I really believe his attitude is softening.*

She signed the message and asked Isaiah to deliver it to Edward's restaurant.

❧

Edward had been interviewing a prospective manager for the restaurant when the message came. He stopped to send an immediate acceptance of her invitation. As soon as he concluded the interview, he went to his apartment. He sank to his knees beside his favorite chair.

"God, I'm not worthy to even call on Your name, but I thank You for giving me an opportunity to make amends for my mistakes of the past. Some men are not so fortunate. My child could have died, and I would never have seen him. If he never accepts me, I can't blame him. But I do want a relationship with him, if it's in Your will. As for Rose, when

I'm with her I have a feeling of contentment I have never known. God, give me wisdom and patience. Amen."

When he rose from his knees, Edward reached for the Bible, which he had laid on the table when he moved into the apartment. He turned the pages, looking for a message to strengthen his faith.

He had always been interested in the plight of the Hebrews after they turned away from God and He had allowed them to be captives in Babylon for seventy years. Edward felt as if he had been in bondage for ten years, since the time he had turned his back on God, blaming Him, as well as the Thurstons, for Martha's death and for the loss of his son. He searched for the promise that God had made to the Hebrews to restore them to their homeland.

Then shall ye call upon me, and ye shall go and pray unto me, and I will hearken unto you. And ye shall seek me, and find me, when ye shall search for me with all your heart.

Edward felt blessed in his soul. He had turned his back on the bondage of sin, and he was on the homeward journey. His observation of the deep faith of the Thurstons had encouraged him to leave his past behind him.

eight

Harry and Lottie still found it difficult to eat in the luxury of Boardman's dining room, but they were slowly adjusting. However, Harry refused to dress up when Edward came to dinner. "I can't do it, child," he said to Rose, when she offered to buy him some dress clothes. "I don't want you to be ashamed of me, but that just ain't my style of livin'."

She kissed his whiskery cheek. "I could never be ashamed of you," she said. "I only wanted to give you the opportunity to have some new clothes. Whatever you wear at my table is acceptable."

"And promise me that when my time comes to die, you won't put no suit on me."

Laughing, Rose said, "I promise, Gramps."

Lottie, however, seemed to anticipate wearing the new dress that Rose had bought for the occasion. She refused to wear a bustle and would put on only one petticoat, but she liked the shot silk, striped rose pink, green, and brown dress. White lace bordered the long sleeves. She entered the parlor tentatively, waiting for Harry's opinion.

"Well, I say, wife!" Harry said in wonder. "Those new duds sure suit you. I ain't seen you look so good since the day I married you."

Lottie actually blushed, and Rose was still laughing at her grandmother's discomfiture when Edward knocked. Sallie hustled from the kitchen to open the door.

Martin had stood in the entrance hall and applauded Lottie's regal appearance. But when the doorknocker sounded, announcing Edward's arrival, he scuttled toward the kitchen. Perhaps noticing the look of dismay on Rose's face, Lottie whispered, "I bet he sits behind the door and listens to every word we say."

Since Edward and Harry had become friendly during their joint effort to protect Rose, conversation flowed easily around the table as they enjoyed Sallie's roast beef, served with new potatoes boiled in their jackets and a variety of vegetables canned the previous summer. Sweet potato pie topped with fresh cream finished their meal.

As they lingered with cups of coffee, Rose led Edward to talk about his mining experiences in Colorado, but Edward was equally interested in Kentucky history, which Harry could supply. While they talked, Rose felt a nudge on her foot. She looked up, and Lottie nodded toward the kitchen. Rose glanced surreptitiously over her shoulder, and she saw Martin's knees in the doorway. He was obviously unaware that he wasn't totally hidden behind the wall.

"That's a small step forward," she whispered to her grandmother under cover of Harry's laughter over one of Edward's stories.

When the meal was over, the four of them went outside. The day had been hot, and they moved chairs to the grassy lawn, where they experienced night falling around them. A slight fog drifted in from the Ohio, barely discernible in the dim light. A steamboat whistle sounded in the distance. While Harry answered Edward's questions about Louisville's history, Rose noticed that Martin sat inside an open window, listening to their conversation.

Edward was clearly enjoying himself, but after an hour, he stood and told them he hated to leave but it was time to go.

"Watch your back," Harry cautioned Edward, as he prepared to leave. "Boardman may be having you shadowed—trying to get you alone."

Her grandfather's comment alarmed Rose. She rose and walked down the sidewalk with Edward. "Be careful."

"I will. I made several enemies in Colorado through the

years, so I've learned to defend myself."

"In a fair fight, maybe, but we know Boardman doesn't play fair. I wish he would leave town. Why is he still hanging around? We leave in two weeks on the showboat's summer tour. I won't rest easy if Boardman is still here."

Edward took her hand. "Thanks for the invitation."

"Consider it an open invitation. The judge gave us a loophole that you could visit upon my say-so. We're going to be busy preparing the *Silver Queen* for sailing for the next several days, so I won't be planning another dinner, but stop in when you want to. Martin was listening most of the evening in the background. He will eventually come around."

"Then you're willing to share him with me?"

"Yes," she answered simply.

"I'd hoped so. That's one of the reasons I've put down roots in Louisville, and I'm trying to be patient."

Noting the sweet tenderness of his gaze, Rose didn't have to ask what his other reason was, and her heart turned over in response. He lifted the hand he held and kissed her long fingers, one by one. "Good night," he said softly and walked away.

❧

The closing day of school was always marked by a program, at which awards were given and students demonstrated some of the things they had learned during the year.

"I've thought of inviting Mr. Moody to the closing exercises," Rose said, when Martin brought the announcement from his teacher. "He would probably enjoy it."

Martin was silent for several minutes, and Rose didn't press him for an answer.

"I reckon that would be all right," he said firmly, "as long as I don't have to talk to him."

"That won't be necessary. But he might like it if you just said hello."

"Oh."

"Mr. Moody doesn't know many people here except our family, and I'm sure he must get lonesome. It would be neighborly to invite him."

Martin slanted a skeptical glance in her direction, and Rose wondered how much Martin really understood about her efforts to include Edward in their lives. She gave a silent prayer for wisdom. As each day passed, she realized how little she knew about rearing a child, especially a boy. God knew what He was doing when He provided for *two* parents.

As she knew he would, Edward welcomed the opportunity to attend the program. When they were being seated in the school's auditorium, Rose arranged for Lottie to sit beside her, and for Edward to sit on Harry's right. She didn't want any speculation among Louisville citizens about what was going on in her life. She had been the brunt of gossip before, for some people had speculated that Martin was her illegitimate child. Perhaps Edward had helped put that particular gossip to rest when he returned and tried to claim the boy.

Rose had bought tailor-made clothes for Martin to wear to the program, and she was gratified to note that he looked as fashionable as the other boys. He wore a dark blue broadcloth waistcoat and jacket, and a white shirt. His black tweed knickerbockers were gathered just below his knees. He wore long black socks and buttoned boots with cloth tops.

Almost two hundred children attended the school, grades one through eight. The program opened with the entire student body singing a few patriotic songs. Each grade was responsible for a short oral presentation, and Martin's teacher had chosen to use a segment from Longfellow's narrative poem, "The Song of Hiawatha," focusing on the young native's childhood. All nineteen boys in Martin's class had been assigned a portion of the poem to memorize.

Rose was so proud as Martin stepped forward from the group and spoke his part.

"Then the little Hiawatha
Learned of every bird its language,
Learned their names and all their secrets—
How they built their nests in summer,
Where they hid themselves in winter—
Talked with them whene'er he met them,
Called them 'Hiawatha's Chickens.'

Of all beasts he learned the language,
Learned their names and all their secrets—
How the beavers built their lodges,
Where the squirrels hid their acorns,
How the reindeer ran so swiftly,
Why the rabbit was so timid,
Talked with them whene'er he met them,
Called them 'Hiawatha's Brothers.'"

As soon as the program ended, Edward approached Rose with a huge grin on his face. "Thank you for inviting me to come tonight. I will treasure the memory of this evening. I owe you so much for giving him a secure childhood."

Rose smiled. "Thank you, again. Why don't you tell Martin you enjoyed it?"

"I would like to, but I don't want to cause him discomfort on this night. Thanks for allowing me to share a small part of Martin's life." He clasped Rose's hand briefly, then left.

Rose watched him go, and when she looked to the stage where the teachers were congratulating the children, she noticed that Martin was watching his father's departure. Was there disappointment on his face? Had he expected Edward to speak to him?

Although Martin still liked to be caressed in private, he was afraid his friends would call him a sissy if he was hugged and kissed in public, so Rose simply put her hand on his shoulders as she congratulated him and the other students.

Rose knew Harry and Lottie were uncomfortable in crowds, and they, too, left after telling Martin how proud they were of him. Once more, Rose assumed the sole responsibility of Martin's upbringing as she mingled with the other parents and children at the reception.

ह

John Boardman always started the showboat tour the first of May, but Rose delayed the departure for a month until Martin was out of school. The two years she and Martin had sailed on the *Silver Queen*, they had caught the boat after its downriver trip. After mooring overnight at Louisville, the boat had traveled the northern Ohio.

Although Rose was eager to take the *Silver Queen* out for the summer, she had some reservations. First of all, she wasn't going on a pleasure trip, as it had been when she had traveled with her grandparents on the *Vagabond*. And the two summers she had worked on the showboat, she had had no responsibility except to obey orders. As the owner and manager of the *Silver Queen*, all of the responsibility was now hers. She doubted that she was equal to the occasion.

She also did not want to be away from Edward for three months. Since Boardman was still hanging around Louisville, she hesitated to leave. He might be waiting for the chance to take over when she was gone. She supposed Edward would continue to keep his eye on her home, but she couldn't expect someone else to accept all of the responsibility.

All day she had been moping around the house, thinking about the carefree days she had enjoyed when she was a girl. After supper, leaving Martin in the care of her grandparents, she walked to the *Vagabond*. Even this brought sadness to her when she reached the vacant boat. It didn't seem the same when her grandparents weren't there to greet her. And she knew that they missed living on the shanty, too. They were sacrificing their pleasure for her, just as she had changed her lifestyle for Martin's benefit.

She sat on the deck of the shanty, took off her shoes and stockings, and splashed her feet in the cool water of the Ohio. She had thought being on the *Vagabond* would make her feel better, but it didn't. She was close to tears when she sensed that someone was watching her. She turned quickly. She wouldn't put it past Boardman to do her bodily harm, and she had been careful not to let him catch her alone. Although she had taken the precaution of lifting the gangplank when she boarded the boat, she was momentarily startled.

Her heart skipped a beat, and happiness overwhelmed her when she saw Edward watching her from the bank.

She smiled, and he asked, "Are you feeling lonely?"

"Morbid is a better word." She stood up and lowered the gangplank to the bank. "Come on over if you like. But I warn you, I'm feeling grouchy."

She motioned him to Harry's rocking chair, and she sat on the deck, her knees flexed, leaning against a bench, her bare feet hidden by her long skirt. "I thought a visit to the *Vagabond* might bring back the days of my childhood when my grandparents and I spent the spring and summer traveling along the river."

"Tell me what those summers were like."

"Our life wasn't much different than it was when we were moored in Louisville, except we were in new settings. We accepted tows from friendly steamboat captains to move around. We stopped at various towns along the river and stayed for a week or two."

"What did you do for money?"

"We didn't need much money. Grandpa caught fish by putting out trotlines at night. He would take the fish to the stores in town, or sell them from house to house. Sometimes he got fresh vegetables or store items, like sugar, matches, and flour, by barter. The steamboats depended on Gramps to provide fish for them. Granny carried herbs with her, and lots of people bought those. At night we hung lighted lanterns on each end of the shanty so the big boats would know where we were. We might stay in a town for two or three weeks when there was a protracted meeting going on at a nearby church. I know it must seem like wasted time to you, but we were happy." Laughing in remembrance, she said, "People called us 'water gypsies.'"

"Did Martin like the river?"

Smiling, Rose said, "He loved it. He learned to swim before he was two years old. But I knew that life was changing, even on the river, and that Martin couldn't live as I had. I worked to pay for his education. I'm thankful to God that I've had the chance to offer him more opportunities than I had. But I'm still happy he spent his childhood on the river. That way, no matter what profession he decides to follow, he will have had the best of both worlds."

"Is this the first summer you haven't traveled along the river on the *Vagabond*?"

"We went last year, for John had died and there was no one to take out the showboat. The two summers before that, Martin and I sailed on the *Silver Queen*. I worked for John in the summer and made enough money to keep Martin in school for another year."

"Aren't you taking the *Silver Queen* out soon?"

"Yes, next week, but it won't be the same. I know John thought he was doing me a favor by willing his estate to me, but it's more responsibility than I think I can handle. To jump overnight from a shanty boat to a mansion on Third Street was quite a change in my social status. If it weren't for Sallie, who has worked in the homes of several rich women, I'd be making more blunders than I do now. And I'm terribly worried about managing the *Silver Queen*. We've been cleaning the theatre and the staterooms on the showboat getting ready for the actors and actresses who'll show up over the next few days." She laughed, a rich, throaty sound that echoed across the water. "See, I told you I was feeling morbid."

🍂

Edward ached to say that he would help Rose with her responsibilities if she would let him, but he couldn't push himself into her business. They had progressed a long way in their relationship over the past month, but he didn't want to add to Rose's frustrations.

"You aren't being morbid—you're just discussing your problems with me. I hope by now you consider me a friend, and that you feel free to talk with me about anything that bothers you."

Without looking at him, she said, "Yes, I do count you as my friend. I don't have many, so I value the ones I have."

"Then as a friend, let me advise you to take one day at a time. That's what I learned to do when I was trying to succeed in Colorado. It seems to me that you've already succeeded at being a 'lady' and a mother. And you will do the same as proprietor of the showboat. If there's anything I can do, please ask me."

"There is something you might do for me. I still employ the same investment firm where John had his money, but I wouldn't know if they're cheating me or not. I've gathered that you have experience in that type of business. Would you mind looking over my records sometime and giving me your opinion? I don't want anyone in Louisville to know the extent of my inheritance, but I would like to know if I have my money in the right place."

Edward breathed a silent prayer of thanks that she trusted him to such an extent. "I'm not without experience along that line, and I'll look at your files when you want me to."

"If you'll walk home with me, I'll give you a copy of my investments. The original documents are in the vault at the bank, but I have copies."

Rose reached for her stockings, put them on, and rolled

them around her ankles. Then she put on her shoes and tied them securely. Out of the corner of his eyes, Edward saw her suddenly stop and blush a bright crimson. He surmised she had realized her societal faux pas at dressing in front of him. He quickly fixed his eyes across the river, hoping she was unaware he witnessed her actions.

Rose rushed on, "I must go home. Gramps might start worrying. I didn't tell anyone where I was going—in fact I didn't know where I'd end up when I started out."

Edward extended his hand, and she grasped it and accepted his help as she stood. He held her hand a moment longer than necessary, but she didn't seem to mind. Rose showed him where to store the gangplank in the small outbuilding. They walked along the waterfront, and she waved to the guard on the *Silver Queen*.

"Have you ever been on a showboat?" she asked.

"No. I know very little about boats."

"We'll be working on the boat all day tomorrow. If you want to come by, I'll give you a tour."

"I'll do that. I've finally chosen a manager for the restaurant, so I'm free most of the time. I didn't know anything about restaurants, either, but there aren't any gold mines in Kentucky, so I thought I'd try my hand as a business owner."

"Did you choose the man who has worked there for several years as your manager?"

"Yes, and I trust him to do what is right."

He walked with her to the house. "I'll see you tomorrow." As she went inside, he realized he was already looking for tomorrow to come so he could see Rose again.

❧

The next day, Rose practiced playing "Camptown Races" on the calliope on the top deck of the tugboat, *Rosewood*. She stopped playing and crossed a catwalk to the showboat, when she saw Edward approaching from a distance. She looked with pride at her "queen." A fresh coat of white paint made the boat appear new, and the large letters of BOARDMAN'S SILVER QUEEN were emblazoned across both sides of the majestic three-deck boat.

Unlike most people, Rose knew showboats like the *Silver Queen* were actually floating barges and did not travel on their own power. A tugboat moved a showboat along the rivers.

All of the Thurstons had been involved in preparing for the boat's departure. At breakfast, Rose had told Martin and her grandparents that she had invited Edward to tour the boat. None of them had made any comment, but Lottie had favored her with a significant glance. Rose realized that her grandparents were well aware of her interest in Edward. Rose asked Harry to meet Edward and bring him to the ship's theatre.

Rose was onstage when Harry found her, bringing Edward with him through the French doors. Martin followed them at a distance.

Harry said, "If you'll show Edward around, I'll go back to swabbin' the deck."

Rose hurried to Edward's side, amused at the shock of discovery on his face as he surveyed the floor-to-ceiling wall hangings featuring scenes of Kentucky's history. His eyes drifted next to the backdrop—a huge painting of the *Silver Queen*, midstream on the Ohio River.

"I'm amazed," he said. "I didn't realize you would have such an elegant theatre. This rivals theatres I've seen in New York City."

"Remember Mr. Boardman came from New York, so he knew how a theatre should look. Let's go onstage and start our tour," she said.

The boat rocked under his feet, and Rose saw that Edward found it difficult to keep his balance for a few minutes. She was able to walk as surefooted as a mountain goat on a high peak.

Edward laughed at his own awkwardness. "The river is definitely in your blood."

Rose and Edward then exchanged significant glances when Martin followed them.

"John had the *Silver Queen* built eight years ago," Rose explained as they climbed the steps to the stage. She sat on a stool and motioned him to an upholstered chair that would be one of the props for the dramas. Martin hunkered down on the steps not far from them.

"You can get an overall view of the theatre from here," she said. "We provide seating for two hundred fifty people—two hundred on the main floor and fifty in the balcony."

"Will you have such a large audience in the smaller towns?"

"The theatre is full the majority of the time, and sometimes people pay for standing room only."

"Apparently this is a profitable business," he said.

Rose smiled slightly, knowing that it was Edward's nature to judge every venture in dollars and cents. "I'm not sure—maybe you can tell me that after you've finished looking over my business accounts. John made his money in the steamboat business, but he sold all except two of them before he died. The showboat was a toy for him in his old age. He really didn't care whether he made any profit on the *Silver Queen*, just so he didn't *lose* money. So I don't expect to make much profit, for it's expensive to operate a showboat. We provide room and board for the actors besides paying them a salary. We have a pilot and four deckhands for the tugboat, which burns a lot of fuel. We take on coal several times as we travel."

"Aren't any showboats self-propelled?"

She shook her head. "I don't think so."

"What's your route?"

"Since we won't be showing as long as John did, we'll go north along the Ohio until we come to the Kentucky River. We'll follow it as far as it's navigable and stop at most every town along the way. Depending on how much time is left before Martin starts back to school, we may go south of Louisville for a performance or two. I plan to tie up the boat soon after the first of September."

Although most of the theatre's seating was general admission, there were a few box seats close to the stage. The stage was four feet wide by fourteen feet long. Several small dressing rooms were backstage. The staterooms and Rose's private apartment were on the second deck. The kitchen and dining area were located behind the staterooms. The pilot and deckhands lived on the *Rosewood*.

Rose explained that the *Rosewood*'s original name was *Tiger Lily*, which she hadn't liked. "I'll never change the showboat's name, but I decided I would put my stamp of ownership on this outfit by changing the tugboat's name."

At the end of the hour-long tour, Rose felt that Edward had a good notion of the showboat's interior, as well as the work involved to put on a show. They climbed the inside stairway to the top deck and entered the pilothouse. Martin had trailed them silently, always in hearing distance, but not close enough that Rose felt inclined to include him in the conversation. When they entered the pilothouse, he joined them and put his hands on the huge wheel, which was locked in place now. He wasn't tall enough to see out the window, but Rose knew the pilothouse had always fascinated him.

Putting her hand on his shoulder, Rose said, "You'll have to grow another foot or two before you can be our pilot."

He climbed up on a bench and looked upriver. "Do you think I can be a boat pilot like Cap Parsons, Mama?"

"I'm sure you can be anything you want to be," she answered. "There's plenty of time for you to decide." Turning to Edward, she said, "The *Silver Queen* can be steered from this pilothouse or from the steamboat. John had his pilot's license, and he steered from the *Silver Queen*. He sometimes let Martin stand on a box and hold the wheel when we were out in the open river."

"That must have been a treat to you, Martin," Edward said. Martin didn't answer. Hearing a sigh and noting the unspoken pain in Edward's eyes, Rose regarded him with sympathy. Perhaps it was right that he should suffer for his actions ten years ago, but she prayed Martin would soon let go of his hurt.

"Cap Parsons has leased his boat to another company for the summer, and he's going to be our pilot. He wants to steer from the *Rosewood*, which suits me. This can be a retreat for the showboat residents when we have a break from our duties. The days do get tedious when we're confined to such a small area."

"This looks like a good place to relax after the day's work is finished."

"Yes, but I learned during the two summers I worked on the boat that there wasn't much time for resting. Everybody had to work. When we weren't rehearsing or presenting the shows, we were studying our lines, helping in the kitchen, or cleaning the boat. I'm hoping to provide more leisure time for the performers this summer."

As they walked down the two flights of narrow stairs to the lower deck, Rose said, "I dread tomorrow when I meet with the cast. I've followed John's example. He didn't hire single women—thinking it led to problems. He took man and wife teams and single men. I've hired two couples and two single men, and they arrive tomorrow. That doesn't sound like many, but with rapid costume changes, the performers can play more than one role in each play. I hope they will accept me as their boss."

"You don't know any of them?"

"No. Sometimes John had performers return year to year, but he thought it led to more interest if he changed some of the cast."

"Remember, I'll help any way I can. I'm going to miss you and your family while you're gone this summer. Thanks for the tour."

Rose watched Edward as he walked away from the showboat.

She had been anticipating the opportunity to leave Louisville and spend a few months on the river. But her pleasure had dimmed considerably. She didn't look forward to the empty weeks when she couldn't see Edward.

nine

Rose worked two more hours after Edward left. She and Martin stocked the ticket office shelves with snacks and gifts to be sold when they started on tour.

Lottie and Harry had already gone when Rose and Martin finished for the day. As they walked toward home, Martin seemed unusually quiet. When they passed the Kentucky Diner, he said slowly, "Mr. Moody seemed to like the *Silver Queen*, didn't he?"

"Yes, I thought so."

"Maybe you ought to invite him to go along and help this summer."

Rose's hands clenched, and in her heart she shouted, *Thank You, God, for Your many blessings!*

Nonchalantly she said, "I imagine he's too busy to spend much time away from the restaurant, especially since he just bought it. But I will mention it to him. I could use his help."

As soon as the evening meal was over, Martin and Isaiah went to the stable. Lottie helped Sallie wash and dry the dishes, and Harry and Rose went to the porch. Harry rocked serenely in a large, cushioned chair.

Rose was amused that her grandfather seemed to be adjusting to town living quite rapidly. He went each morning to check the trotlines for fish, and he still delivered his catch to his best customers, but she believed he found a more leisurely life pleasant. This made her happy. After all her grandparents had done for her and Martin, she hoped that she could use Boardman's legacy to make their waning years easier.

Rose sat on the floor near her grandfather, so she could look up into his face. "When Edward came for a tour of the *Silver Queen* today, Martin followed us every place we went. When we were walking home, he suggested that I invite Edward to sail with us on the showboat."

Harry wagged his head wisely. "I figgered the boy would come around. Are you going to ask him?"

"I don't know. I wanted to talk to you about it first."

"You like Edward, don't you?"

"More than I should," Rose admitted.

"I don't agree to that. Edward has changed a lot in the past month. He's a good man."

"I hesitate to ask him to go with us. I don't want him to feel obligated. Do you think he would be interested?"

"Does a dog bark?" Harry said, followed by his cackling laughter.

Slightly annoyed because Harry was treating a situation so lightly that mattered a great deal to her, Rose scowled at him. "What is that supposed to mean?"

"It means that it's high time you open your eyes, girl. Do you think Edward has been hanging around here just because of Martin? He likes the boy, but you ought to see how he watches *you* when you ain't lookin'. I don't know if he even knows it himself, but it 'pears to me that the man is in love with you."

"Gramps!" Rose said, although her grandfather's words caressed a spot in her heart that had been lonely for a long time.

Cackling again, Harry rocked back and forth in his chair.

"And that would please you?" Rose asked.

"Yes, child, it would please me. My time on earth can't be much longer, and when me and Lottie are gone, I'd be glad to know that you have a man to share your life. Edward ain't without faults, but he *is* a good man. He's shown that a dozen ways since he's been here."

"I know that. I appreciate his attitude about Martin and the many things he has done for me."

"But don't you take no man out of gratitude! That ain't the way to have a good marriage. Lottie and me have had a good life—lovin' each other through thick and thin. And there's been more thin than thick, I can tell you that. But them things don't matter when there's love in the home. I don't want you to settle for nothin' less."

Wiping her eyes, Rose said, "Now you've made me cry."

"Cryin' is good for a body onct in a while," Harry said. "Washes out some of our doubts. But about askin' Edward to sail with you on the showboat, I'd say do it. Matter of fact, I've been worryin' some about all of us leavin' for the summer, with that Boardman feller still hangin' around here. If Edward will go with you, I think Lottie and me had better stay in Louisville and keep our eye on your property and ours. I won't fret about you if Edward is on board—he strikes me as the kind of feller who would stay calm in a cyclone."

"Very well," Rose said, standing. "I'll go talk to him now. You can explain to Granny."

Looking at the western sky, Harry said, "It's gonna be dark before long, and you'd better not be out by yourself."

"If Edward doesn't walk home with me, I'll hire a carriage. I'll go upstairs and get my bag so I'll have some money."

"Well, keep your eyes open."

❧

Rose had eaten in the Kentucky Diner many times, but she hadn't been inside since Edward had bought it. The manager recognized her and offered to show her to a seat.

"No, I'm looking for Mr. Moody. Is he here?"

"He's been upstairs in his apartment for about an hour." Pointing to the rear of the restaurant, he said, "You can use the inside stairway, if you like."

"Would you mind asking him to come down and talk to me?" Although she had no qualms about seeing Edward alone in his apartment, Rose tried to avoid anything that would reflect adversely on her reputation.

"Not at all," the manager agreed.

He signaled for one of the waitresses to take his place behind the reception desk and turned toward the steps. He soon returned, followed by Edward, who looked somewhat alarmed.

"Is something wrong?" he asked immediately.

"No, but I have some business to discuss with you."

He motioned toward the dining room. "Would you like to have something to eat?"

She shook her head, refusing his offer. "I've already eaten. Could we walk instead?"

He opened the door for her. Sensing that she wanted privacy, he said, "There's a courtyard behind the restaurant. Shall we go there?"

"That will be fine."

When they were seated, shoulders touching, on a bench in a small white gazebo in the courtyard, Edward said, "What has happened?"

"I hesitate to mention this, and please don't agree if you aren't interested. Martin suggested that we invite you to go with us on the showboat tour."

A happy, eager look flashed in his brown eyes. "I accept," he said.

With a happy heart, Rose smiled. "Just like that? No details about how long we'll be gone? No questions?"

He took her right hand and squeezed it gently. "Just one question—do *you* want me to go?"

She looked away from him—fearing what he might read in her eyes. "Yes, I do," she said quietly.

"That's all that matters. I've been feeling very sorry for myself that I wouldn't have any of the Thurstons around this summer. Louisville would have been empty without you."

"I discussed this with Gramps, and he says if you go with us on the boat, he will stay in Louisville to keep an eye on the

Vagabond and my home. I suppose he thought if you were in Louisville, you would watch over things."

"Which I intended to do, and I agree that either Harry or I should stay in town while the other one goes on tour."

"He's still worried about Boardman."

"And so am I. He's hanging around town for no good reason."

"What about your restaurant?" she asked, motioning toward the building.

"I have full confidence in my staff, but I can return to check on them occasionally, or have Harry do it."

"It's always possible to come home for a brief visit on another boat. And there's train service from Frankfort to Louisville."

Rose realized that Edward was still holding her hand, and she started to remove it from his grasp, but he tightened his hold.

"Do you know what this means?" Edward asked softly.

"That Martin is starting to accept you?"

He tenderly squeezed her hand. "That and other things, but we'll have the whole summer to discuss them."

Because her heart was flopping in her chest like a headless chicken, Rose freed her hand, saying pertly, "There won't be as much time as you anticipate. Don't think you're going on a pleasure cruise—everybody works on a showboat."

They stood, and he said, "It's getting dark. I'll walk home with you, and you can tell me what I'll have to do to earn my keep."

As they strolled through the gathering dusk, Rose said, "While I walked here to see you, I tried to think what your duties could be. I knew well enough that you wouldn't be content to spend the summer without some responsibilities."

He laughed. "You know me too well," he admitted. "But what can I do?"

"I'm too inexperienced to manage everything like John did,

so I intend to delegate some of the responsibility. Since you're in the restaurant business, would you be in charge of feeding the showboat's workers? That would mean buying food when we dock, and although it's customary for all the women on board to take their turn preparing food, I believe it would be an advantage if you would hire a cook and two other men or women to work in the kitchen, who would also be available as stand-in performers. Your duties would include supervising these workers, too."

"I had more people applying for work in the restaurant than I needed. I'll contact them and find three workers for you."

&

When Edward and Rose reached the house, she asked, "Do you want to talk to Gramps about anything? He may still be on the porch."

But the porch was empty.

"I won't come in now," Edward said. Without asking permission, Edward leaned forward and kissed her forehead. She smiled at him and went inside. He walked slowly toward his apartment with a light heart.

Although it appeared that a closer relationship with Rose was a possibility now, he wondered what might have happened if he had stayed in Louisville when his wife died. From what Rose had said, it must have been several months before they knew if Martin would live. If he had waited until the boy was well enough to travel, would he have taken him and gone to Colorado? Or would he have fallen in love with Rose then and been content to remain in Kentucky? Remembering his love for Martha at that time, he doubted he would have had room in his heart for any other woman. But had he missed ten years of Martin's life, as well as almost that many years of being happily married to Rose?

Edward knew it was pointless to wonder what might have been, but he realized now how dreary his life had been without the love of a woman. Since this summer might bring him the things he wanted most in life, he could be patient a little longer.

⁂

When Rose was ready to leave the house the next morning, she realized she must have looked frightened when Lottie took her into the parlor and motioned for Rose to sit on a chair. Rose suppressed a grin, remembering the few times during her childhood when Lottie had found it necessary to reprimand her.

Favoring Rose with a stern look, Lottie put her hands on her waist. "Rose, I want you to march down to that boat and let those actors know right away that you're the boss. In the Bible, Paul the apostle did some plain speakin' when he was advising Timothy, his young son in the Lord. He said, 'For God hath not given us the spirit of fear; but of power, and of love, and of a sound mind.' As Paul said to Timothy, I'm telling you today—*don't be afraid*."

"I don't know that it's fear, Granny. It just isn't my nature to be giving orders."

"Then you will have to let God change your nature. I don't mean for you to bully the people onboard the *Silver Queen*, but don't let them put anything over on you, either. God, through John Boardman, has given you this opportunity, and you've got the strength to handle it."

"Thanks for the prodding," Rose said as she stood up, and in a whining, childish voice, added, "Kin I go now, Granny?"

Lottie swatted Rose on the slight bustle she was wearing. "Don't get sassy with me, missy," she said. "You're still not too big for me to bend you over my checkered apron and paddle you."

Laughing, Rose said, "I don't believe you know how to do that. You've threatened me before and didn't carry through on your threats. It's too late now."

Lottie followed her out on the porch. "Mind what I say, now."

"Look after Martin," she said. "He's eager to leave on the

showboat, but he's worrying about being away from Tibbets all summer. He's persuaded Isaiah to take him riding this afternoon. See you tonight."

When Rose reached the *Silver Queen*, she saw that Edward hadn't wasted any time. He was already at the wharf supervising the unloading of several cartons of food items that would last until they arrived at another large city. He had bought all of the staple items, such as flour, sugar, lard, and canned goods. Fresh vegetables, fruits, meat, and milk would have to be purchased at towns along the way.

"I'll give you a check to pay for everything," Rose called, waving to him as she went onboard and walked to the small room near the ticket window that John Boardman had used for his office. None of the performers had arrived yet, and that gave her time to rally her defenses.

She had hired these people, sight unseen, and she hoped that their résumés had been correct. Since she hadn't considered anyone who had traveled on the *Silver Queen* when she worked as a kitchen helper, she probably wouldn't have much trouble. She would have less resentment from people who had never known her before her social and financial rise in the world.

The morning went better than she had expected, and Rose attributed the success to her conviction that Sallie and Lottie had spent much time on their knees praying for her. As she discussed their duties with the entertainers, Rose often heard Edward's voice as he instructed the workers about unloading the foodstuffs and where he wanted them stored. He obviously wasn't any novice at giving orders. She was heartened by knowing he would be available to help her. All she had to do was call him, and he would be with her immediately.

His nearness furnished the strength she needed to tell the newcomers what she expected of them. She showed them to their staterooms, and since Edward was bringing the cook and her helpers on board today, she told the performers that their supper would be served on the boat. She gave them copies of the two plays they would be presenting during the summer, asking them to study the scripts and be ready for rehearsals on the first full day of traveling.

Since showboat audiences loved plays that included a villain trying to woo the heroine, she had chosen *Becky Goes to the City*. The drama featured a country girl who leaves her betrothed behind on the farm to go to the city to make enough money to help them get started in life. She takes a job in the villain's factory, and at first she succumbs to his smooth talk and almost forgets her beloved. When the villain kidnaps her and takes her to a lonely cabin, where he intends to keep her until she agrees to marry him, the hero comes to the rescue.

The second play, *'Til We Meet Again*, was a Civil War play. Although Kentucky had not left the Union during the war, there were many Southern sympathizers in the area. The heroine's boyfriend goes to fight with the Confederacy. While the Union army is in Kentucky, a Union soldier courts her. Three years pass, and the heroine hears nothing from her beloved. She's almost on the point of marrying the Union soldier and moving north when the hero returns. She immediately knows that her heart lies with the Confederate soldier.

When she finished for the day, Edward waited for her on the lower foredeck. "I rented a wagon to haul the groceries to the boat. Do you want to ride home with me?"

"I probably need the walk, but I am tired, so thanks for the offer."

"You've done a lot of walking up and down stairs today. That's all the exercise you need."

"Yes, sir," she said, her eyes twinkling.

A slight blush spread across Edward's face. "Sorry, I didn't mean to be giving you orders."

"Oh, I don't mind. I need somebody to tell me what to do. Granny sat me down and told me how to behave before I left home this morning."

"Harry stopped by today and gave me orders, too. If anything happens to you this summer, I get the idea that they will hold me personally responsible."

"He shouldn't have done that," she said, frowning. "I've already given you enough responsibility. What did you tell him?"

"I asked him if he thought I had to be ordered to look out for you."

Slanting a glance toward him, she said, "I'm afraid to ask what he answered."

"He didn't even answer me. He laughed knowingly and went on his way."

Rose allowed Edward to hold her arm and help her into the wagon. He then untied the horse, took his seat, and flicked the reins. The mare turned her head and looked at him. He touched her back with the tip of a whip. She didn't move.

"Giddup," he shouted, and the mare plodded away from the wharf.

"Apparently the stableman is trying my patience by always renting this animal to me. Surely there are better horses available for hire. "

Because the day had gone well, Rose was in a roguish mood, and she asked mischievously, "She won't take orders from you, either?"

"No," Edward said. He touched the horse's flank with the switch again, but it didn't change the animal's gait. "When we get back from this tour, I'm going to buy a horse. I did a lot of riding in Colorado."

As the horse plodded slowly away from the river, Rose sighed deeply. "Maybe the mare is as tired as I am," she said. "But as far as I can tell, we're ready to set out two days from now."

"At what time?"

"Around noon. That will give time for any last-minute

preparations or to take care of things we've forgotten."

"How did the interviews go?"

"All right, I guess, but I won't know how good the performers are until we've put on a show or two. They all came with good recommendations, so I pray everything will turn out for the best."

"How many performers do you need?"

"I hired six adults. Stephen and Naomi Buckley and their twelve-year-old daughter, Becky, who will do children's parts. The other couple is Ranson and Hannah McCall. They not only act, but sing, as well, and he can play the calliope. They've had experience on showboats in the New Orleans area. There are two single men, Anthony Persinger and Luke Melrose. For some reason I don't feel satisfied with Luke. He doesn't seem as open about his past as the others, but I'll not judge him until he gives me some reason to."

"I won't interfere with your work, but remember I'll be available to help you."

"Thanks. I'll count on that. I've put the performers in the three staterooms on the right side of the boat. Your quarters will be on the same side as the stateroom Mr. Boardman always used. Martin and I will stay there. The cook and kitchen helpers' rooms will be between ours."

When they arrived at Rose's home, Edward helped her out of the wagon. She was sad when he refused her offer to have supper with them. Martin stood at the front door waiting for her, so she told herself she was glad Edward had not kissed her again, but in her heart she knew that was not the truth.

❧

Since Louisville was the *Silver Queen*'s home port, a large crowd gathered on the riverfront to watch the boat's departure. Red, white, and blue pennants waved from the top railing of the showboat. Captain Parsons had steam up on the *Rosewood*, and black smoke poured from its smokestack. Ranson McCall was playing the calliope as loud as he could.

Edward recognized "Oh, Susanna," which was a popular song in Colorado. Ranson soon swung into "Old Folks at Home," and "Beautiful Dreamer," two other Stephen Foster songs.

Lottie and Harry had come aboard with Rose and Martin, helping to carry their satchels. Now they had gone ashore and stood watching the activity. To Rose, they looked rather lonely and forlorn, and she knew they would have liked to go on the journey. Martin was running around the walkways, too excited to stay in one place very long.

When Captain Parsons blew the whistle for departure, Edward came to Rose's side.

"All of Louisville's residents must be here to watch us leave," he said.

"Not all of them, but it's nice to have such a send-off. And the performers are excited, too. I hope we're this happy when we return at the end of the season."

"Why wouldn't we be?"

She shrugged her shoulders. "Lots of things can happen during a trip like this. Thirteen of us will be confined on this boat, besides Captain Parsons and the deckhands on the *Rosewood*. We might get on each other's nerves. Two years ago, one actor quit right in the middle of the season and walked out—leaving Mr. Boardman in the lurch."

"Don't worry," he said, placing his hand lightly on her shoulder.

"I'm not much. I'm sure you noticed that there's one on-looker I'd rather not have seen." She motioned toward Walt Boardman, who leaned against a wharf building, close enough for Rose to detect the sneer on his face. "I'm worried that he's remained in Louisville. I'm not concerned for my property as much as I am about what he might do to Granny and Gramps."

"When Boardman didn't leave town, I hired a man to shadow him. So far, he hasn't done anything. And Harry and I have arranged for several men to keep an eye on my restaurant, your home, and the shanty boat. Besides, Harry knows how to look after himself. He won't be caught napping. And if Boardman follows the boat, I'll be around."

"You'll never know how much comfort that gives me," she said softly, touching his arm lovingly. He pulled her close for a moment.

The showboat moved slowly away from the dock as the *Rosewood* gave it a gentle nudge. A shout erupted from the shore.

"We're on our way," Rose said. Martin loped toward them and snuggled close to Rose. She put her arm around his shoulder.

"It's so much fun, Mama. A summer out on the river. This is almost as good as being on the *Vagabond*."

Rose exchanged glances with Edward. The shanty compared poorly to the *Silver Queen*, but the riches she had inherited hadn't changed Martin. His early years had molded his character.

Too excited to stand still, Martin raced away from them.

"After all," Edward said quietly, "he was born on the *Vagabond*."

"And since he may inherit two steamboats, as well as a showboat someday, perhaps it is good that he loves the river."

As they headed downstairs, he said, "I've been looking over your investment portfolio, and I'm impressed not only with John Boardman's business acumen but also with your brokers. I noticed that when Boardman sold several of his steamboats, he invested in railroad stock."

"And you believe that is wise?"

"Absolutely. Just as I think it was wise for him to keep a couple of steamboats. There will always be boats traveling these rivers, but railroads will be vastly important in the development of this country, especially the West. I've invested in railroad stock, too."

"Thanks for checking this for me."

"When we have more time, I'll sit down with you and explain facts and figures. I'll help any time you want me to, but you should understand what you have. Also, when we return to Louisville, I'll go with you to the investment company if you like."

"Thanks. That's one less worry on my mind. During the summer, I hope running the showboat is all the responsibility I have."

ten

As soon as the boat was out of sight of Louisville, Anthony Persinger, whom Rose had chosen as their director, called the cast together, and they started rehearsing. Their first scheduled stop was at Madison, Indiana, and they had to be ready to perform. He had chosen *Becky Goes to the City* as the play they would present first.

Since in emergencies every person on the boat might be needed for back-up performances, Rose invited Edward to go with her and Martin into the theatre for the first rehearsal.

"After a week or two, when the cast members know all of their parts, we won't have to do much practicing," Rose explained to Edward. "But at first everyone is tense. Anthony has had some experience in directing. He's single and has never worked with any of the other performers, so he won't be likely to play favorites with the roles he assigns. But we need back-up performers for each role, which involves all of us who have other duties. You can listen and decide which role you want to play," she said with a smirk on her face.

Edward stared at her. "Me? Stand up in front of two hundred people and act?"

"Everyone pitches in to help in an emergency," she insisted. It was pleasant to see that some things could discomfit Edward. "Even the cook and the waitresses pull extra duties occasionally."

Knowing she was enjoying his discomfiture, Edward said sternly, "If I remember right, acting wasn't mentioned in my job description."

Anthony Persinger came by their seats, and Rose asked,

"Anthony, do you have any standby parts where Edward could fill in?"

Anthony looked Edward up and down. "Why, I'm sure we can use someone like you. You will be an excellent standby for the hero in both dramas."

He rifled through the papers he held and handed Edward a couple of scripts. "Study these in your spare time, and I'll have you read some of the portions to me privately to see how you fit in."

Still amused at the consternation exhibited on Edward's face, Rose teased, "If he doesn't work out for the hero, he might make a good villain."

Edward groaned. "This is going to be a long summer."

❧

Advance notices had been sent ahead, and the Madison townspeople were expecting the showboat. Several miles downstream, Ranson started playing the calliope, and when the showboat rounded the curve in the river and the town came into view, the hills echoed with the sounds of "My Old Kentucky Home."

The *Rosewood* edged the showboat toward land, and the deckhands jumped across the water to secure both the tugboat and the *Silver Queen*. At least a hundred cheering, excited people waited on the bank.

Standing beside Rose on the top deck, Edward said, "I'm surprised there are so many people in this town."

"There will be more here tonight when we show—they'll come in from the country when they hear the calliope. The sound travels for several miles. Are you going uptown with us this afternoon for the parade announcing the performance?"

"If you want me to."

"Are you always this docile?"

"No. Enjoy it while it lasts. But after all, you are the owner of this boat."

"I keep forgetting that."

His eyes conveyed a message that Rose couldn't interpret. "So do I," he replied. "I'm going onshore now to buy a supply of fresh meat and ice. We'll need it before we cast off in the morning. What time is the parade?"

"Midafternoon."

"I'll be back by then."

ॐ

Captain Parsons had volunteered to go with Edward and introduce him to the local merchants. They passed a long line of people waiting to board the *Silver Queen*.

"Why are they waiting now?" Edward asked the captain.

"Some of them will buy tickets for tonight's show. Others are just curious to see if any changes have been made since last year. The coming of the showboat is the most exciting thing that happens to some of these people all year."

Glancing over his shoulder, Edward noticed that Rose stood near the gangplank, greeting people as they boarded the boat.

"I hope all of this responsibility isn't too much for Rose."

With a short laugh, Cap Parsons said, "Don't worry none about that gal. You've not seen her grow up like I have. She'll still be goin' strong when the rest of us have had enough."

"Her grandparents gave me orders to look out for her."

"They told me the same thing. Nothin's gonna happen to her."

When Edward and Parsons returned, the sightseers were all gone, and the performers were ready to go into town to advertise their show.

Edward and Luke Melrose walked in front of the others, carrying a large banner advertising the event. Rose played her banjo. Ranson McCall played a trumpet. Stephen Buckley pounded on a drum. Becky Buckley and Martin gave pieces of wrapped candy to the children. The other performers shook hands with the spectators who lined the streets and handed out show bills. They gave twenty free tickets to children.

The show was scheduled to start at seven thirty, and the ticket office opened an hour earlier. The gangplank had been lifted to keep the guests off the boat until they were ready.

৯

By curtain time, all of the seats were filled, and for half-price tickets, some stood on the deck and peered in through the windows. Rose stood on the main deck, with Martin beside her, welcoming her guests until the theatre was almost filled. Then she went backstage to chaos.

Acting the part of a big-time producer, Anthony Persinger was tearing his hair, haranguing the cast, and wandering up and down the walkway between the stage and dressing rooms, his eyes wild and his voice strained.

"We'll never pull this off," he said. "We're not ready for opening night. No talent at all in this group. Why did I ever agree to be the director?"

Even though the Buckleys had not worked with Anthony before, with a grimace Naomi said in an aside to Rose, "This is usual opening night behavior for a director—think nothing of it. The show will be wonderful, and then he'll strut around the showboat as if he pulled off the whole thing single-handed."

Rose shared the woman's laughter, for during her two years of working with John Boardman, she had learned that actors were generally a volatile group. But opening night was always tense until the performers got the audience's reaction to their presentation.

Only a few minutes were left before opening time, when Rose peered through a small opening in the curtain, and a flicker of apprehension spread through her. Walt Boardman and another man were walking down the aisle into the box-seat area, close to the stage. Was he following the *Silver Queen*? Would he try to harm the performers?

Rose hurried backstage. "Do any of you know where Edward is?" she asked the assembled group.

"I saw him in the back of the theatre a few minutes ago," Hannah McCall said.

"Delay opening the curtain for a few minutes until I get back," she said to Anthony.

"Oh, no," he cried and threaded his fingers through his thick mop of black hair. "We can't be late on opening night."

"Most of these people have no idea what time it is. I'll be back soon and welcome everybody." Anthony's agonized pleas to start the show immediately followed Rose as she hurried offstage.

Martin and Becky were perched on the stairs that led from backstage to the theatre floor. They wanted to see all the backstage action.

"Have you seen Mr. Moody?" Rose asked.

Martin pointed to the rear of the theatre where Edward stood like a sentinel guarding the room. As she hurried toward him, she marveled that Martin always seemed to know where Edward was. He saw her coming and hurried toward her.

"Boardman is in the theatre," she said.

Her face was clouded with uneasiness, and he smiled reassuringly. He put his arm around her shoulders, gave her a gentle squeeze, and held her close for a moment. She melted into his embrace, gaining courage from his strength.

"I saw him. I'll keep my eye on him. Go on with the show." He motioned to the opposite side of the theatre where one of the deckhands stood. "He's on guard, too. Don't worry."

"Why do you think he's here?"

"Probably to intimidate you. Don't let him do it."

Thankful for the quiet assurance Edward gave her, her confidence was restored. Rose lifted her hand and caressed his cheek. Smiling her thanks, she hurried back to the stage. She signaled to Stephen and Ranson in the orchestra pit. Stephen played a Viennese waltz on the violin, and when he finished,

Ranson presented a drum roll to indicate the program was beginning. The two musicians hurried backstage.

Rose breathed a prayer for help as she parted the curtains and stepped out. The audience grew silent, except for a trill of excitement among the spectators eager for the show to get underway.

Although she had done some bit parts during her two years on the showboat, Rose had never in her life given a speech. The silence of the audience frightened her. She was determined not to look toward Boardman, so she glanced in Edward's direction. He saluted and threw her a kiss.

Encouraged, she spoke earnestly to the crowd. "Welcome to the premiere presentation of the *Silver Queen*'s 1886 summer tour. Tonight's performance is dedicated to the memory of John Boardman and his contributions to the showboat industry.

"Let's bow our head in a moment of silent prayer as a tribute to our friend, who died a little more than a year ago." In the silence that followed, Rose detected a hissing sound from the box seats where Boardman was seated. Knowing that Edward was on guard gave her the courage to keep her eyes closed through the prayer.

"God, we thank You for the life of John Boardman, who provided several years of meaningful entertainment to the residents of Kentucky. This opening night's performance is dedicated to him. We also pray Your blessings on this audience as well as the performers. Amen."

Rose raised her head, and with a genuine smile of welcome, she said, "It's a pleasure to be your hostess tonight." With a sweeping gesture of her arm, she said, "Let the show begin!"

The performance went well. When the cast appeared onstage for the grand finale, an a cappella rendition of "My Old Kentucky Home," the audience collectively rose to its feet and sang with them. A deafening applause came simultaneously with the closing words of the popular song.

When the last guest left the boat, the cast gathered in the kitchen to celebrate with coffee and ate heartily of the fruit pies the cook had made for the occasion. After an interval, Rose went to the top deck, taking Martin with her. Edward followed them, asking, "Do you mind? Or would you rather be alone?"

"No, sit down," she said as she sank wearily to a bench. Edward sat on a bench opposite hers. Martin leaned over the rail and peered into the water. A cold breeze blew across the boat, and Rose asked, "Martin, would you mind going to our stateroom and bringing my black shawl?"

"No, Mama, I'll get it," he said, clambering down the steps.

"What about Boardman?" Rose asked when Martin was out of hearing. She didn't want the child alarmed unnecessarily.

"I kept my eyes on him, expecting him to throw something at the actors. You probably heard a few boos coming from his section, but he didn't do anything else. I followed him when he left the boat. He had horses stabled in town, and he and his buddy rode away. I don't know anything more than that."

"He's up to some devilment."

"I think so, too. But we're on guard."

"Should I warn the cast?"

"Not yet. We'll see if he comes back. It may be that he was curious about a showboat performance and this was a one-time visit."

"You don't believe that, do you?"

He grinned. "No, but I wanted to ease your mind if I could."

Martin returned with her shawl, and she wrapped it around her shoulders. They were silent, listening to the gentle lapping of the river on the boat. A cacophony of croaking frogs surrounded them. An occasional splash in the water indicated the presence of fish. Insects droned quietly in the background. Martin leaned over the railing, watching the shimmer of the showboat's lights across the water.

Edward looked upward. "We have quite a display of stars tonight. Do you see the Big Dipper?"

"I know very little about the stars," Rose said, "although I've loved a starlit night since I was a child. Gramps showed me where the North Star was, but not much more."

"If you can find the North Star, it's not difficult to locate the Big Dipper." He stepped behind Rose and pointed upward as he talked. "The Big Dipper has seven stars in it. The two stars in the front of the cup point to the North Star. The Little Dipper is part of a group of stars, and it's very important as an indicator of the north, because the North Star is in the end of the Little Dipper's handle."

Rose was conscious that Martin had left the railing and was standing beside Edward, hanging on to his words. He had never been this close to his father before.

"Apparently you've studied this," Rose said.

"I spent four years at Harvard. I majored in history and business subjects, but I took some classes in astronomy for pleasure. People have been intrigued by the mystery of the heavens since the beginning of time."

"One of the earliest Bible verses I learned was, 'When I consider thy heavens, the work of thy fingers, the moon and the stars, which thou hast ordained; what is man, that thou art mindful of him?' I always think of those words when I'm out on a night like this."

"Mama, wonder what the big white group of stars means?"

Edward put his hand on Rose's shoulder and squeezed it gently. Rose sensed that he was pleased that Martin was joining in their conversation.

"I don't know," Rose answered. "Perhaps Mr. Moody can tell us."

"That's called the Milky Way, Martin. I've looked at that group of stars through a telescope, and there are many more stars than we can see. There are clouds of dust particles and gases that lie throughout this galaxy. On clear, dark nights like this one, it appears as a milky-looking band of starlight stretching across the sky. The longer I study the universe, the more I realize how much is yet to be discovered."

"You'll have to talk to us about this again, Edward," Rose said. "But it's time for bed now."

They walked silently downstairs and along the walkway to their rooms. They spoke quietly so as not to awaken any of their shipmates who were already sleeping. At Edward's door, Rose said, "Good night."

A long-held look with Edward spoke volumes about their feelings for each other and about the slight indication that Martin was slowly accepting his father.

Martin was sleepily removing his clothes by the time Rose entered the stateroom. He knelt beside the cot for his prayers. "God bless Mama, Grandpa, Granny, and. . ." He paused. Rose wondered if he was going to include Edward in the prayer, but Martin continued, "And Tibbets. Help me to be a good boy. Amen."

In the darkness, Rose undressed, donned a night shift, and crawled into her bunk. She supposed that Martin was sleeping until he said, "Mr. Moody knows a lot, doesn't he?"

"Yes. He's a very smart man."

Martin said no more, and soon his even breathing indicated that he had gone to sleep.

છ

As they continued showing on the Ohio River, all went well on the *Silver Queen*. Boardman didn't return to the showboat, and Rose became optimistic that he had left Kentucky.

Then irritating things started. They arrived at Carrollton to find only a few people on shore waiting for them. The man Rose had hired to tack up advance notices hadn't been seen.

Three rowdy spectators showed up when they stopped at Worthville, threw eggs at the performers, and started a fight in the balcony. The culprits escaped before the men on the boat or the police could apprehend them.

The next morning when Captain Parsons couldn't start the engine on the *Rosewood*, he discovered that sand had been poured into the engine. It was obvious that someone was trying to hamper their performances. Rose became concerned for the safety of the crew members and performers.

Captain Parsons and Edward discussed the situation with Rose, both convinced that Boardman was responsible for the vandalism, although they hadn't seen him since opening night. The three also considered the possibility that some of the employees could be responsible, for the damage to the *Rosewood* must have been done at night after the gangplank had been lifted. Luke Melrose, one of the actors, was a loner, and although he did his acting well, Edward proposed that he might have been hired by Boardman to disrupt the performances. But Parsons was more inclined to suspect one of his deckhands, a man he hadn't worked with before.

When the *Rosewood* was ready to sail again, Rose called the crew and performers together. She explained Boardman's enmity toward her and that she blamed him for the harassment. She didn't want to endanger their lives, and she gave them the opportunity to vote whether or not to continue the tour.

"I've been in danger before," Stephen Buckley said. "If we stop now, we'll be out of work, for it's too late to sign on with any other troupe this late in the summer. All of us can be on guard now that we know there's a problem."

Edward noted to Rose that Luke Melrose was the only one to vote for discontinuing the tour. He protested that they were making a mistake and that they might be in danger.

"That's well enough for you to say," Ranson McCall countered. "You don't have a family to support. My mother is keeping our two daughters for the summer, and I need some money to provide for them."

"I still think it's a mistake," Melrose said.

"Does that mean you want to leave?" Rose asked with a

mixture of relief and misgiving. She should have hired an extra performer to step into the breach if someone quit the tour.

"Not yet," Melrose retracted. "But I value my life, and if we have any more trouble, I may leave."

"Then we'll plan to go on as usual," Rose said.

The next day, Stephen and Naomi Buckley became sick with vomiting and diarrhea. Both were too weak to leave their beds. Anthony paced the theatre floor.

"Why did this have to happen?" he cried, tearing at his hair until it hung in strings over his forehead. "Never again will I agree to be a director. I can't bear the loss to my prestige when we have inferior acting."

Edward and Rose walked in on him, and he peered at them between the strands of hair.

"What are we going to do?" he shouted. "*What* are we going to do?"

Stifling a smile, Rose said, "We can use the standby performers. We're fortunate that we haven't had to do so before this. Two years ago a couple walked out on Mr. Boardman, and the stand-in actors performed the rest of the season."

Anthony slumped into a seat and lifted his hands upward. In an agonized voice he said, "Don't even mention such a thing. If this tour is a disaster, my reputation will be ruined. I might as well jump in the Ohio to spare myself the embarrassment."

"Perhaps we should cancel the show until the Buckleys get better," Rose suggested mischievously.

"No! No!" Anthony said. "We will cope." He headed toward the stage.

"While he's coping," Edward said, "I should tell you that someone may have put a large portion of castor oil in the Buckleys' food. They were late coming into the dining room last night, and they served themselves from a pot of stew that had been left on the stove. There was a little left in the pot this morning. The cook took a taste, and she thinks somebody had added something to the food."

"But why wouldn't they have noticed the taste in the food?"

"Perhaps because it was hot when they ate it—I don't know."

"That would have been done by someone on these boats," Rose said.

Before they could discuss it further, Anthony came back. "My decision has been made. The show must go on. Rose, you will play the heroine in *'Til We Meet Again*. Edward, you can be the hero. Your lines are not long, but you will have to pretend to be in love with Rose."

Lowering his left eyelid at Rose, Edward said, "That will take a lot of acting."

Rose felt her face flushing, and she frowned at him. But Anthony took Edward seriously. He wrung his hands and took a turn around the theatre, gesticulating wildly.

"Oh, I know. You don't strike me as being very romantic, but I don't have any other choice."

"I'll do my best," Edward said meekly, and Rose pinched his arm.

"Oh, I forgot," Anthony shouted in agony. "Can you sing? That closing scene requires a duet."

"Get your banjo, Rose," Edward said. "I've listened to Stephen and Naomi sing 'Beautiful Dreamer' several times. Let's give Anthony an audition."

Rose picked up the banjo and strummed a few chords. "Since you have such a low voice," she said, "I'll sing the melody, and you take the harmony part."

They sang a few lines, and Rose was surprised at the skill in Edward's voice. He had a natural, pleasant speaking voice, but that didn't necessarily mean he could sing. Rose strummed a final chord and looked at Anthony.

"Well, if you can act as well as you sing, we'll be all right," he said grudgingly. "I only hope you don't mess up the production and ruin my reputation."

"I'm sure your reputation will still be intact after the show," Rose said dryly.

Anthony was a good director, and Rose had learned to live with his pessimistic attitude. She knew that Edward's and her voices blended well, and would be a hit with the audience, but Anthony was meager with his praise.

Rose and Edward spent the rest of the morning studying their parts, and the afternoon rehearsal went well. During the evening presentation, they performed well. Edward seemed to find it difficult to forget himself and put himself wholeheartedly into the hero's role, but he spoke distinctly.

Fortunately, he didn't appear to develop stage fright. In the first act, when the hero was leaving to serve in the Confederate Army, they received spontaneous applause, and Rose heard some sniffles from the audience. Edward didn't appear onstage again until the closing scene. Three years passed, the war was over, and when nothing had been heard from the hero, the heroine believed that he had died. On the eve of the day she was to give the Union soldier an answer, she sat on the porch, her head in her hands, mourning her dead love.

Edward, portraying the hero, stepped onstage and watched Rose for a few minutes. He snagged her attention by singing, "Beautiful dreamer, wake unto me."

Rose jumped up from the chair, hand at her breast, and ran toward him.

"Oh, my love," she cried. "I thought you were lost to me. I have missed you so much."

"The years have been long, my dearest one. Every night I prayed that I would live to see you once more. God has answered my prayer. I will never leave you again."

"Thank God, you've returned. I thought you had died and

that my heart had been buried with you."

Edward bent over her. During the rehearsal, he had not kissed her but had drawn her into a close embrace as the curtains had closed.

Rose forgot that she was in view of two hundred people playing a role, and she sensed that Edward, too, had forgotten they weren't alone. She stood on tiptoe to touch her lips to his. His lips pressed against hers, then gently covered her mouth. The moment was electrifying, and when Rose gasped, Edward backed away from her quickly.

Apparently in a daze, Edward forgot his closing line.

"You're supposed to say you love me," Rose whispered.

Holding her eyes with his, he said loudly and sincerely, "I love you. I love you."

The audience roared their approval, but Rose wasn't ready for the emotions his caress had roused. She picked up her banjo, strummed a few chords, and forced herself to forget what had just happened. She blended her voice to his in the timeless words of Stephen Foster.

> "Beautiful dreamer, queen of my song,
> List while I woo thee with soft melody,
> Gone are the cares of life's busy throng,
> Beautiful dreamer, awake unto me."

After the play was over, Rose went through the motions of bidding good-bye to her guests with a smile on her face, but she was confused, and her mind rioted at the implication of Edward's gesture. She was convinced that the caress had surprised Edward as much as it did her.

Unwilling to deal with her rioting emotions, she avoided Edward the rest of the evening and went to her room as soon as the last guest left the showboat. Long after midnight, Rose still lay wide awake on her cot. The boat was quiet. Finally, tying a full-length robe over her nightgown and leaving the door of her stateroom open in case Martin awakened and called for her, Rose wandered to the front of the walkway. She leaned on the banister overlooking the water, hoping for peace from the conflict within her heart. The gentle lapping of the waves against the hull didn't calm her tonight.

❧

Edward couldn't sleep but lay on his bunk, fully dressed. He had left his door ajar hoping he might have an opportunity to see Rose. He hadn't intended to kiss her, but he had actually forgotten he was acting a part. It had seemed right to tell Rose that he loved her, and the caress was automatic— something he had wanted to do for days.

When he heard her door open and Rose's steps on the walkway, doubting his welcome, Edward walked quietly in the direction she had gone.

Seemingly deep in thought, Rose didn't turn around until Edward was directly behind her. She started to move away, but he gently gripped her arm.

"Are you trying to avoid me?"

"Yes, I guess am."

"Rose, we have to deal with what happened. Why put it off?" When she didn't answer, he added, "I suppose I should say I'm sorry."

"Are you?"

"No."

She shivered, and he led her toward a nearby bench that offered some protection from the cool breeze. "Let's sit for a while. I saw your door is open, so we can hear Martin if he calls. I didn't intend to kiss you. I simply forgot for a moment that it wasn't real."

She put her hand on his arm. "It's all right. I'm not sorry either."

"I automatically did what I've wanted to do for a month. Did I embarrass you?"

She shook her head, and he sensed that she was crying.

He took a handkerchief from his pocket and wiped away the tears.

"I've wondered a few times what it would be like to have you kiss me. But it stirred feelings I can't deal with now. We have several more weeks on this showboat, together every day. It might have been better if we could have remained just friends, without any disturbing, hidden emotions."

"Maybe. I promise to exert more self-control from now on. I don't want to add to your worries."

"Do you think Martin is warming to you?"

"He seems to be."

"If he senses anything between us, it might upset him very much. I don't know how I can handle a sulky child with everything else confronting me. Even though I wanted to carry on this showboat tradition to repay John for having faith in me and giving me his estate, I don't think I'll ever take this responsibility again."

"Couldn't you lease it to another person? You could still own the boat and let it carry the Boardman name."

"I'll consider that before another season. I know my limitations, and I'm not authoritarian enough to manage this boat, the actors, and the crew. I'm constantly fretting whether I'm making the right decisions."

She didn't resist when he dropped his hand over her shoulder and drew her closer. If he got his heart's desire, Edward had an answer for her problems. He had no difficulty handling authority, but he didn't want her to agree to marry him because she needed a business manager. He wanted more—much more—from Rose. He wanted her heart.

She turned to him and grinned. "Since we're going to be circumspect during the rest of the voyage, will you kiss me again before we go back to our rooms?"

"Happy to oblige," he said, affection in his voice. He kissed her forehead, the tip of her nose, and her closed eyelids before he lingeringly kissed her soft lips.

"I'll have this to remember when I'm overwhelmed with decisions," she said. "But now we must get some sleep. Captain Parsons intends to weigh anchor early tomorrow morning."

eleven

The next morning, Edward suggested to Rose that they should hire a night watchman. "I'm worried about all of us sleeping without anyone on guard."

"This is so frustrating to me," she said. "All the years we traveled the river in the *Vagabond* we never locked a door, day or night. And nothing was ever bothered. Same way with the *Silver Queen*. All John did was pull in the gangplank when the crowd left after the show."

"It's just a suggestion. But if you do decide to hire a guard, he can share my stateroom and sleep during the daytime."

"I've been checking the books, and we're barely breaking even on expenses and ticket sales now. Delays like we had when the *Rosewood* was vandalized were costly. You said you had looked over my investment portfolio. Am I making enough money so I can afford to take a loss on the showboat tour?"

He couldn't control his burst of laughter. "You'll never miss it. John Boardman was obviously a shrewd businessman. But I'll pay for the night watchman. It will be worth it for my own peace of mind."

"I'd rather pay for it myself, but whom shall we hire?"

"I'll talk to the sheriff when we come to the next county and let him suggest someone. In the meantime, I'll patrol at night. I'm used to going without sleep. I can manage."

But when Luke Melrose learned that Edward was standing guard, he insisted on spelling him every other night. Edward still suspected Melrose, and he stayed on guard even when the other man was on duty. His vigilance paid off one night when he heard whispering on the lower deck. He removed his shoes and eased down the stairs.

"Melrose," a man's voice muttered, "see to it that you're on guard two nights from now when you're docked at Frankfort."

Edward had only heard Walt Boardman's voice a few times, but he felt sure Boardman was the man speaking.

"I'm sorry I ever got involved in this mess," Melrose said. "Miss Thurston is a fine woman."

"Do what I tell you, or I'll see that you're sent back to New York to face that robbery charge."

The two men moved out of hearing, and Boardman soon left. Edward hurried back to his stateroom and spent the rest of the night wondering what they should do. It was obvious that Boardman had known Melrose in New York where he was a wanted man. Edward was tempted to confront Melrose and force him to implicate Boardman. Or was it best to post a watch and catch Boardman in whatever scheme he was hatching against the showboat? Was it risky to wait? Although he wanted to spare Rose the worry, it was her right to make the decision about this new problem.

After breakfast the following morning, Edward asked Rose to accompany him to the top deck. He looked carefully in the pilothouse and checked behind every pile of rope or equipment where someone could be hiding. Then he invited her to sit beside him on a bench facing the stairway.

Quietly he told her what he had seen and heard the previous night. As he talked, Rose's shoulders slumped in despair. Edward was tempted to propose to her on the spot. If she accepted him, he would be more inclined to offer his advice.

"Oh, Edward!" she said finally. "If Boardman would promise to leave Kentucky and never come back, I'd gladly give him everything I inherited and be done with it. I didn't want John's legacy in the first place. I learned through the years with my grandparents that it didn't take riches to be happy and to live a worthwhile life. I guess it's impossible to change a shanty boat mentality."

"Rose," Edward said sternly, "don't give up. We grow through adversity. There is nothing wrong with a shanty boat mentality. Your background with Harry and Lottie turned you into the wonderful woman you are today. I'm willing to take the responsibility for dealing with Boardman, but you *are* capable of doing what has to be done."

"I know," Rose said. She paused for a few minutes. "I'm acquainted with the sheriff of Franklin County. He and John were friends, and he hung around the showboat during the time we were docked at Frankfort. If we go to his office to enlist his help, Boardman might become suspicious. But I expect the sheriff to be at the dock to welcome us when we arrive in Frankfort. I'll talk to him privately, and he'll help us. If we can catch Boardman in the act of sabotaging the boat, or whatever he means to do, maybe that will take care of the problem."

"That's my girl," Edward said approvingly, gently rubbing the tense spot between her shoulder blades. "What do you want me to do?"

"One of us should keep Martin in sight all of the time. Boardman might try to do something to him. You didn't overhear what they're planning to do?"

"No. They moved out of hearing, and I didn't dare go any closer, for I didn't want them to know I had overheard their plans. I'll also watch Melrose. If Boardman is holding his knowledge of Melrose's crime over his head, he's probably the one who sabotaged the *Rosewood*. He might do something else to one of the boats."

"Perhaps I should have checked the background of the performers more thoroughly. If there is a next time, I'll be more careful. But that won't help me now. I can't dwell on my past mistakes."

Edward took her hand. "That's something I've had to come to terms with, too, Rose. When I think of how I acted and what I said to you and Lottie the night my wife died,

I feel lower than a snake. What I did then ruined ten years of my life. But for weeks now, since I've started reading the Bible again, I keep turning to Paul's words in the book of Philippians. Although the apostle's situation differed from mine, I keep thinking of his words, 'This one thing I do, forgetting those things which are behind, and reaching forth unto those things which are before, I press toward the mark of the prize of the high calling of God in Christ Jesus.'" His eyes darkened with misery, and his brow moistened.

"Don't, Edward. You don't have to explain anything to me."

He shook his head. "I have to speak. I'm trying to put the past behind me because I've asked God to forgive me. I believe He has, so I want to ask your forgiveness for the long years you had to struggle to raise Martin alone. Also for the worry I caused you when I returned to Louisville."

Rose put her hand over his mouth. "Since God has forgiven you, do you think I can do any less? I don't regret one minute I've spent with Martin. I should thank *you* for giving me the opportunity to have ten years of his life. He's been a joy to me and my grandparents. I'm only sorry that you missed his early years. I forgive you, and I don't want you to ever mention it again. You must eventually have a talk with Martin, but the slate is wiped clean between you and me."

"But the only way I can put the past behind me is to look toward the future. I believe the highest calling I can strive for is to be a good husband and father. I can't see any future without you and Martin in it, and when the time is right, I hope all three of us will know it."

"We will," Rose said and lifted her face for his kiss. He didn't touch her, but leaned forward and pressed a light caress on her lips.

&

When they arrived at Frankfort, as Rose had expected, Sheriff Collins was on hand to meet the *Silver Queen*. He was among the crowd who hurried onto the showboat to see if any changes had been made since the year before and to meet the new performers.

Watching carefully to be sure that Melrose didn't hear her, Rose stood close to the sheriff, a rugged man in his midfifties. Quietly she said, "I'm expecting some trouble here. See me privately."

The sheriff was as shrewd as he was competent, and he walked on without acknowledging Rose's comment. He circulated in the dining room where the cook was serving coffee and cookies to the crowd, chatting with the actors.

Soon Collins stopped beside Rose, and in a moderate voice he said, "Miss Rose, we're thinking about starting new regulations next year regarding reserved space along the waterfront so we can be sure to accommodate everyone. Can you spare me some time?"

"Sure, come into the office."

They walked to the office, and Rose closed the door. "What's up?" the sheriff asked.

Quickly Rose sketched Boardman's arrival in Louisville and his claim on John Boardman's estate.

"We've had some trouble with harassment in a few towns," she said, "and Mr. Moody, my associate, overheard Boardman plotting with one of our actors about something to happen here in Frankfort. We're going to be on guard, but if the police can catch Boardman in this plot, I might get rid of him once and for all."

"We aim to keep the law in this county, and I'll have some of my men watching day and night." He motioned to a grove of trees on the bank. "That's a good place to keep out of sight."

"Mr. Moody will volunteer to work both nights, and if Melrose insists on guarding one of those nights, we'll guess that is the night to expect trouble."

"I'll come to the show tonight, and you can say either 'tonight' or 'tomorrow night' when I pass by. But I'll probably post a guard both nights, just to be sure."

When Melrose insisted on guarding the second night, Edward agreed. And when the first night passed without incident, Rose and Edward were convinced that Boardman and Melrose would strike the next night.

After the show, while the actors greeted guests, Edward moved from the showboat to the *Rosewood*. He told Captain Parsons that he wanted to spend the night on the tugboat, but he didn't want anyone to know about it. Parsons favored Edward with a shrewd look, and Edward had the feeling that the captain would also be on guard.

While the performers were still in the dining area, Edward went to the second deck and placed a roll of blankets in his bunk to resemble a body. He didn't know that this precaution was necessary, but it was possible that Melrose might be suspicious and check on him. Walking in the shadows as much as possible, he crossed from the showboat to the tugboat on the catwalk. He eased into a supply room that had a tiny porthole facing the front of the showboat and quietly closed the door.

After an hour of waiting, quiet settled over the two boats. Edward walked out on the deck of the *Rosewood*. Fortunately, it was a moonless night, and in his dark clothes, he didn't think he could be seen. He sat on the deck with his legs flexed and peered through the railing.

In the faint glow from one of the lighted lamps, he saw Melrose sitting on a coil of rope on the foredeck of the *Silver Queen*. The gangplank had been pulled in for the night, but Luke could quickly lower it into place across the six feet of water separating the boat from the bank.

Edward didn't dare strike a match to look at his watch, but he knew when several hours had passed. Had he been wrong? Had he misunderstood what Melrose and his companion had said? His legs were numb from holding them in one position for hours. He moved backward to stretch his legs, and fighting the desire for sleep, he yawned.

He became alert at once when Melrose stood, picked up the gangplank, and quietly lowered it toward shore. Two figures moved stealthily down the bank. Edward crawled toward the showboat and eased his way to the larger craft. In his need for quietness, it took longer than he had anticipated to reach the main deck of the *Silver Queen*.

When he smelled kerosene, he launched his body into a run and sped toward the front of the showboat. A slow blaze burned near the ticket office, and he recognized Melrose as the figure pouring kerosene on the blaze. Edward tackled him, and Melrose fell backward into the fire he had just started.

Melrose screamed as the can of kerosene exploded in his hands and ignited his clothing. Edward jumped away from him to avoid being burned. Melrose's screams increased, and pandemonium broke loose. Sheriff Collins and a deputy ran across the gangplank, cutting off the escape of Boardman and his ally.

"Fire! Fire!"

&

Rose, who hadn't undressed and had spent the long hours sitting on her cot, ran from her stateroom and down the steep steps. She witnessed Edward pick up the screaming Melrose and pitch him into the shallow water near the bank to extinguish the flames. Within minutes, the *Rosewood*'s crew and the residents of the showboat formed a bucket brigade.

Momentarily, Rose stared at the spreading flames, knowing how quickly the boat could be destroyed, but she was more concerned about Edward than the boat. She saw that trapped between the sheriff and Edward, Boardman snarled like an animal at bay. Edward rushed toward him. Boardman fired a gun at close range, and Edward collapsed. The sheriff clouted Boardman on the head, and while he was staggering from the blow, the sheriff handcuffed him. The deputy captured his accomplice.

"Edward!" Rose shouted and rushed to him. Exerting all of her strength, she turned him over, and the last embers of the fire illuminated a bloody hole in his chest.

"God," she whispered, "I can't lose him now."

Stephen Buckley knelt beside them and searched for a pulse in Edward's wrist. "He's still alive."

"Let's get him to a doctor right away," Rose said. "Sheriff Collins will tell us where to go."

Wildly she turned to Stephen. "Will you stay with the other performers and be sure the fire is out? Captain Parsons, have your deckhands bring a cot, and we'll carry Edward to the doctor. I'll tell Martin where we're going."

Ranson McCall and Anthony Persinger knelt on the deck trying to get Luke Melrose's attention. The water was shallow, and the flames were out now, but Melrose still floundered in the water. They threw a float board to him, but he ignored it. Ranson jumped in the water and lifted Melrose's body to the deck of the showboat. The fire must have burned him badly, for Melrose writhed on the deck of the boat, groans accompanying each move he made.

"He'll need a doctor, too," Captain Parsons said.

"Take care of it then. I'll go see about Martin," Rose said.

Martin had slept through all of the commotion, but he sat up in bed rubbing his eyes when Rose rushed into the stateroom. She explained what had happened and said, "I'm going to the doctor with Edward, but Naomi and Becky will stay with you."

Martin jumped off the cot and reached for his clothes. "I want to go with you, Mama," he said.

"Hurry and dress then." Although she couldn't bear the thought of Edward dying, she knew if he did die, he would want to see Martin.

The next hours passed in a daze for Rose, and she only focused on the important details. She and Martin followed as the men carried Edward and Melrose up the bank and into town. The sheriff arranged for two wagons to haul them to the nearest doctor. Since the doctor's home was less than a mile away, they took the injured men there instead of to a hospital. Rose and Martin rode on the wagon bearing Edward's body, and for reassurance, she kept her hand on his pulse.

After they carried Edward to a bedroom, she and Martin waited in the living room of Dr. Shively's home. His wife brought coffee for her and a glass of milk for Martin. He finally went back to sleep, leaning heavily against Rose.

Rose monitored the passage of time by listening to a striking clock on the mantel. Two hours passed before Dr. Shively entered the room and motioned for her to follow him. He set Rose's mind at ease immediately. "As far as I can tell, the bullet missed any vital areas, but it lodged inside his right shoulder, and I had to remove it. That caused him to lose more blood and will delay his recovery. But he has a strong body, and I can't see any reason why he won't recover after being laid up for a few weeks."

"Thank You, God," she said, her lips trembling. Taking the doctor's hand, she said, "And thank you, too, Doctor."

Mrs. Shively had worked with Melrose while her husband operated on Edward, so the doctor left Rose to sit beside Edward while he checked on the burned man.

Rose pulled a chair to the bed and took Edward's hand. Since Edward always seemed full of vitality, it was heart wrenching to see his immobile body. But in his unconscious state, he seemed younger, more vulnerable, more like he had looked the first time she had seen him.

Martin knelt beside the bed for a long while, but finally fatigue overcame him and he curled up on a blanket Mrs. Shively had placed on the floor. Daylight filtered into the room, and with the sun shining, Mrs. Shively came to extinguish the lamp. She invited Rose to come to the kitchen for some food. When Rose refused to leave Edward, the doctor's wife brought her a cup of coffee and a hot biscuit.

"I'll feed the little tyke when he wakes up," she said, "but I'm afraid your mister won't feel like eating for a while."

"Mr. Moody is a friend," Rose said, hastening to correct the assumption that Edward was her husband.

The doctor's wife blushed, and she stammered, "I'm sorry. I just supposed. . ."

"Don't be distressed. It's only natural you would assume that." Smoothing back Edward's hair, Rose added, "He's a very *dear* friend, however."

Mrs. Shively looked from the patient to Martin, lying asleep on the pallet. Rose noticed that in sleep Martin resembled his father more than at any other time. Mrs. Shively must have been curious, but she asked no questions.

"Yes," Rose explained, "they are father and son but were separated at Martin's birth. I adopted Martin when he was three years old. His father only came into our lives in April, and Martin hasn't accepted him yet. We need your prayers," she added.

Embracing Rose's shoulders, the motherly woman said, "You will have them."

Edward's even breathing and the return of color to his face encouraged Rose. In midmorning he stirred restlessly and moaned in his sleep. Believing he was regaining consciousness, Rose whispered to Martin, "Wake up, son." Martin yawned and wiped his eyes, but he scurried off the floor and crawled up on the bed at Edward's feet. Rose knelt beside the bed and wiped Edward's face with the damp cloth Mrs. Shively had provided. Her arm rested lightly on his bandaged shoulder when Edward opened his eyes. When he shifted his shoulders, he visibly winced. Rose knew his wound was painful even if it wasn't fatal.

He blinked his eyes and focused on her face. She leaned over and kissed his cheek. Martin moved forward, and Edward looked toward him.

"Have I died and gone to heaven?" he asked in a weak

voice, so unlike his usual vibrant tone that Rose's eyes filled with tears.

"Not this time," she answered, squeezing his hand. "You won't get away from me that easily."

"Are you feeling better, Mr. Moody?" Martin asked.

"Yes, thank you, Martin." His eyes were unusually bright when he turned to Rose. "What happened?"

"Boardman shot you. The bullet missed your lungs and your heart, but it was embedded in your shoulder. Dr. Shively had to remove it. You'll be laid up for a few weeks, but you're going to get well."

"Did the *Silver Queen* burn?"

"No. The men put out the fire. I've been here with you, so I don't know how much damage there is. Now that I know you will be all right, I'll go to the showboat and find out what has to be done."

"What happened to Boardman and his crew?"

"Melrose is in the next room with a sheriff's deputy guarding him. Sheriff Collins stopped in an hour ago and told me that Boardman broke away from him and jumped in the river, trying to escape. He was in handcuffs and apparently wasn't much of a swimmer, for he drowned. They did recover his body. They questioned the man who was working with Boardman, and he's implicated Boardman in all of our trouble this summer. As soon as Melrose is well enough, he'll be sent back East to face the charges against him."

"Why did he team up with Boardman?"

"Walt knew him in New York. There's a warrant for Luke's arrest in the East, and Walt told him that if he didn't help destroy the *Silver Queen*, he would report him to the authorities."

"I pitched him in the water to put out the flames."

"Yes, I know. He will go to jail as soon as the doctor releases him."

"Mama told me how you fought those mean men," Martin

said. "You were very brave, Mr. Moody."

Before Edward could reply, Dr. Shively came into the room. "So," he said, "you're awake and able to talk."

"Yes," Edward said, "thanks to you."

"Partly to my skill, but mostly because you are strong and healthy." The doctor looked sternly at Martin and Rose. "Now you two need some rest. My wife will fix beds for you."

"Thank you," Rose said, "but I want to go to the showboat and see how things are there." She leaned over and kissed Edward's forehead. "We'll be back this afternoon."

Martin reached out his right hand, and with a slight grin, Edward grasped the tiny hand with his left one and shook it gently. "Mama and I will pray for you, Mr. Moody."

ᔌ

After Rose and Martin left the room, Edward reflected on what had just occurred. He couldn't believe what Martin had said to him. *It's a beginning.*

Edward silently thanked God that He had seen fit to entrust Martin into Rose's care. He had always thought it was chance that he had found a midwife when Martha went into premature labor. But had God ordained his meeting with the Thurstons? Had He been orchestrating his life and theirs during the past ten years to eventually bring them together again? It was a humbling thought, but Edward knew it was true. Surely the day was soon approaching when Martin would accept him and the three of them could become a family. *God, grant me patience,* he prayed.

twelve

Until she crossed the gangplank and stepped on the deck, Rose didn't notice any damage to the showboat, but the impairment was soon evident. A sizeable hole had burned in the floor beside the ticket window. The fire had crept up the stairway to the balcony, and several of the steps were charred beyond use. The door to the office was blackened, but a quick look inside indicated that the safe and other files hadn't been damaged.

She had to make some immediate decisions, and she wished her grandparents were here to tell her what to do. She couldn't ask Edward for advice when he was so ill. It was up to her, and she prayed for guidance.

Holding Martin's hands, she moved toward the dining area, where she found the performers. They were eating breakfast, but she glimpsed despair on their faces. They rushed toward them when they saw Martin and her in the doorway.

"How is Edward?" Anthony asked.

"Recovering, thanks be to God," Rose said.

"We're sorry for your misfortune. None of us had any idea that Luke was working against you," Ranson said.

"I realize that." To the cook Rose said, "Please bring a cup of tea for me and some breakfast for Martin." She sat down and motioned for all of them to gather around her.

"I did a lot of thinking during the night," she said. "Without knowing the extent of the damage to the boat, I was sure that we couldn't continue the show this season."

They nodded forlornly, and she added, "But you will all receive your full pay."

"Oh, no, Miss Rose," Persinger protested. "We don't expect

that. This tragedy isn't your fault."

"Anthony, by now all of you have heard about my youth. I spent twenty-seven years of my life without much money. My grandparents and I lived from season to season. And I know that's the same way with you. I don't even have to consider between losing some money and helping you and your families make it through the next few months. I'm sure John Boardman would have made this same decision."

Naomi Buckley sobbed and sat down in a nearby chair, pulling her daughter to her side.

"We won't start back to Louisville until Edward is ready to travel, and I don't know how long that will be," Rose continued, "so all of you performers must make arrangements to leave when you can. There will be other boats along, or it might be quicker if you take a train into Louisville. It's possible you can still find some employment for the rest of the summer. I don't know what will happen during the next year, but if we do take the *Silver Queen* out again, I'll keep you in mind."

She turned to the cooks and the deckhands. "I want you to stay with the boat and travel back to Louisville with us. You'll also get full pay."

"Do you want us to go ahead and clean up the mess, Rose?" Captain Parsons said. "We might as well do something while we wait."

"The boat is insured, and the insurance adjusters will want to look over the damage. Do we need to make repairs now?"

"We'll have to fix that hole in the deck before we go back out on the river," he insisted.

"Then do what you think is necessary," Rose said.

❧

The performers left the next day on the train, but it was a week before Edward was brought to the showboat in a wagon. Putting him on a mattress, Captain Parsons and the three deckhands carried him onboard.

Rather than taking him to the second deck, Rose had made a bed for him near the stage in the theatre. Soon Captain Parsons gave the departure whistle, and the *Rosewood* nudged the showboat out into the river. From the top deck of the *Silver Queen*, Rose played "God Be with You 'Til We Meet Again" on the calliope, as Frankfort citizens waved from the bank. She made a few mistakes, but no one seemed to notice.

❧

Still weak from his wound, Edward slept often during the first two days. Martin volunteered to read to him one morning, and he accepted with gratitude, pleased with how well the child read. But though Martin was friendly, there was a wall of reserve that Edward couldn't break through.

After Martin left to pester Captain Parsons into letting him steer the tugboat, Edward complained to Rose, "Will he ever accept me as his father? Do we have to wait forever? I love you, and every day that passes, I think it's another day we could be happy together. I want to be your husband, even if I can't be Martin's father."

"I love you, too, and I won't let Martin's attitude keep us apart any longer. He has to learn to forgive. As soon as you are well, I want to get married. I don't know how, but God will work out the details."

"Sorry I can't seal our promise with a kiss."

"There isn't anything wrong with me," she whispered. Rose leaned over him and lowered her lips to his. With his left arm, Edward pulled her tightly against him and deepened the caress.

❧

On the last night before they reached Louisville, after Edward was asleep, Martin and Rose stood on the top deck, listening to the drone of the insects and looking at the stars.

"Mama, are we going to take Mr. Moody home with us so Granny can look after him? He might get lonesome in his apartment."

Rose moved to a bench and pulled him down beside her. "Martin, I need to talk to you about this. There's only one way we can bring Edward into our home to live—and that's as my husband."

His shoulders tensed, and she didn't press the point for a few minutes. She had carefully avoided saying that Edward would be his father. "Do you like him enough to agree to that?"

After a minute passed, he slowly nodded his head.

"No," she said firmly. "A nod isn't enough. I don't want any misunderstandings between us. Edward and I love each other. If we're married, that means Edward will be sharing my life—my bedroom, my business decisions, and all that I do. My love for him will not alter how much I love you, but he *will* be as important to me as you are. You look me in the eye and tell me how you feel about it."

He swallowed, and he sniffed a little. She knew it was a difficult decision for the child to make, but finally he lifted his head and looked at her. His lips trembled a little when he said, "It's all right, Mama, I'll share you with Mr. Moody."

Thank You, Lord, Rose prayed silently. She kissed Martin tenderly. "You've made me very happy, son."

Rose went immediately to tell Edward. She knew they had won a major battle, but the war wasn't over yet.

Edward disagreed with the plan to take him to her home until he could go there as her husband.

"I'll be perfectly comfortable at the apartment," he said. "Mrs. McClary will come in every day. The Bible teaches that we should shun all appearance of evil, and we don't want any gossip attached to our marriage. I can be patient now that I know we will soon be together. Let's plan a honeymoon. Where would you like to go?"

"Somewhere on the river," she said.

"How does New Orleans sound?"

"Good, but we would be gone a long time."

"We'll talk it over with Harry and Lottie as soon as we

get settled at home and see if they'll watch out for Martin."

&

"It's an excellent plan," Lottie said at once. "We can take Martin with us on the *Vagabond*. Now that Boardman ain't a threat, Harry has been chomping at the bits to take off in the shanty. We can spend a month out on the river. Harry will keep Martin so busy, he won't miss you. We can be back before his school starts, and that will give you and Edward time for a weddin' trip."

"Granny, my life has been like the flow of the river— sometimes peaceful, other times a bumpy ride. And I've been tossed on the waves. But in God's own timing, He brought Edward and me together."

"I pray that you and Edward will find the happiness you deserve."

"We will, Granny. We will."

&

The wedding took place in Rose's home with only the Thurstons and Sallie and Isaiah present. Instead of a formal wedding dress, Rose chose a blue silk garment that would be suitable as a traveling dress when they boarded the packet boat for the trip to New Orleans. Dr. T. T. Eaton, pastor of the Walnut Street Church where Rose and Martin attended, came to the house to perform the ceremony.

Martin had been quieter than usual at the wedding, but he didn't shed any tears, and as Edward and Rose stood on the deck of the boat waiting for departure, he waved to them. It was the first time Rose had been separated from Martin, and she felt a tug at her own heart when the boat left the wharf. She knew the separation was necessary, not only for Edward and her to bond in the special meaning of marriage, but it also would be good for Martin to understand right away what sharing her with Edward meant.

The days on the boat and the week in New Orleans strengthened the love that Rose and Edward had for each other. They spent hours strolling around the streets of the old town, marveling at the mixture of Spanish and French architecture. They tried out all of the famous restaurants. They spent one day at a nearby plantation purchasing an Arabian gelding for Edward.

Rose sent word when they expected to return. The day of their arrival, her grandparents, Martin, Sallie and Isaiah, and many other acquaintances waited for them. As they walked down the gangplank, Martin ran to Rose, threw himself into her arms, and kissed her, something he hadn't done in public for a year or more. Her arms tightened around him because she had missed him, too.

When she released Martin, he turned to Edward and held out his hand. "Welcome home, Mr. Moody."

With a resigned look at Rose, Edward shook his out-stretched hand. "Thank you, Martin."

The Arabian hadn't been happy about the boat trip, and the trainer Edward had hired to make the journey had a difficult time controlling the animal during the unloading.

Martin was delighted with the spirited horse. "I want to ride him, too," he shouted.

"You'll have to be content with Tibbets for a while," Rose said.

The trainer led the horse away from the landing, and they had quite a following before they reached Third Street. Martin was more excited over the new horse than he was over the gifts they had bought for him.

"Probably Tibbets is going to seem pretty tame to him now," she told Edward after they had gone to their room and were preparing for bed. She expected trouble keeping Martin away from the animal, but she didn't expect trouble to come as soon as it did.

❧

Rose and Edward awakened to a frantic pounding on their bedroom door.

"Mr. Edward. Miss Rose," Isaiah shouted. "Martin is riding the new horse."

Edward yanked on his clothes quickly, but Rose simply tied a robe around her nightgown and hurried to the paddock. Martin sat bareback on the Arabian, which looked around at the child as if he wondered what the small object was doing on his back.

When Edward and Rose arrived at the paddock, the trainer came running from the stable. "I turned the horse out to let him get over his frisky ways before I rode him," he cried. "I didn't know the boy was even around here. He must have mounted him from the fence."

"Martin, get off that horse, right now!" Rose shouted.

The horse moved away from the fence, and the child looked terrified as he monitored the long distance to the ground. The horse switched his tail and shook his shoulders as if to rid his back of the foreign object. Martin's face turned white, but Edward opened the paddock gate and stepped inside.

"Careful, Martin," he cautioned. "I'll come closer to help you."

"You'd better let me do that, Mr. Moody," the trainer said. "That horse is skittish."

Edward shook his head. As he neared the animal, the Arabian started a fast walk around the paddock. As the horse's pace increased to a lope, Edward moved closer.

"Daddy," Martin cried, terror-stricken, "I'm afraid. Help me."

Rose was quick to catch the significance of Martin's call, as if the child had been thinking of Edward as his father for a long time.

When the horse made another circle and neared him, Edward shouted, "Jump, son! Jump! I'll catch you."

Martin had been holding to the Arabian's mane, but when the horse circled again, he let go and leaped toward the ground. Edward grabbed him and took a rolling plunge away from the horse. The trainer ran into the paddock and grabbed the Arabian by the mane.

"Daddy! You saved me!"

Rose ran toward Edward and Martin, tears in her eyes and laughter in her heart.

Two little arms encircled Edward's neck and a moist kiss was planted on his cheek. Hugging Martin tightly in his arms, he started crying.

Kneeling beside them, Rose spread her arms around the two people she loved most in the world. They were a family at last.

A Letter To Our Readers

Dear Reader:
In order that we might better contribute to your reading
enjoyment, we would appreciate your taking a few minutes
to respond to the following questions. We welcome your
comments and read each form and letter we receive. When
completed, please return to the following:

Fiction Editor
Heartsong Presents
PO Box 719
Uhrichsville, Ohio 44683

1. Did you enjoy reading *Where the River Flows* by Irene Brand?
   ❏ Very much! I would like to see more books by this author!
   ❏ Moderately. I would have enjoyed it more if

   _____

   _____

   _____

2. Are you a member of **Heartsong Presents**? ❏ Yes ❏ No
   If no, where did you purchase this book? _____

   _____

3. How would you rate, on a scale from 1 (poor) to 5 (superior),
   the cover design? _____

4. On a scale from 1 (poor) to 10 (superior), please rate the
   following elements.

   _____ Heroine   _____ Plot
   _____ Hero   _____ Inspirational theme
   _____ Setting   _____ Secondary characters

5. These characters were special because? _____
_____
_____

6. How has this book inspired your life? _____
_____
_____

7. What settings would you like to see covered in future
   Heartsong Presents books? _____
_____
_____

8. What are some inspirational themes you would like to see
   treated in future books? _____
_____
_____

9. Would you be interested in reading other **Heartsong
   Presents** titles? ❏ Yes ❏ No

10. Please check your age range:
    ❏ Under 18   ❏ 18-24
    ❏ 25-34   ❏ 35-45
    ❏ 46-55   ❏ Over 55

Name_____
Occupation _____
Address _____
City, State, Zip_____

Hearts♥ng

Presents

Great Inspirational Romance at a Great Price!

Heartsong Presents books are inspirational romances in
contemporary and historical settings, designed to give you an
enjoyable, spirit-lifting reading experience. You can choose
wonderfully written titles from some of today's best authors like
Peggy Darty, Sally Laity, DiAnn Mills, Colleen L. Reece,
Debra White Smith, and many others.

When ordering quantities less than twelve, above titles are $2.97 each.
Not all titles may be available at time of order.

HEARTSONG
PRESENTS

If you love Christian romance...

$10.99

You'll love Heartsong Presents' inspiring and faith-filled romances by today's very best Christian authors...DiAnn Mills, Wanda E. Brunstetter, and Yvonne Lehman, to mention a few!

When you join Heartsong Presents, you'll enjoy four brand-new, mass market, 176-page books—two contemporary and two historical—that will build you up in your faith when you discover God's role in every relationship you read about!

Imagine...four new romances every four weeks—with men and women like you who long to meet the one God has chosen as the love of their lives...all for the low price of $10.99 postpaid.

Mass Market 176 Pages

To join, simply visit www.heartsong presents.com or complete the coupon below and mail it to the address provided.

✂ -

YES! Sign me up for Heartsong!

NEW MEMBERSHIPS WILL BE SHIPPED IMMEDIATELY!
Send no money now. We'll bill you only $10.99 postpaid with your first shipment of four books. Or for faster action, call 1-740-922-7280.

NAME _____

ADDRESS_____

CITY_____ STATE _____ ZIP _____

MAIL TO: HEARTSONG PRESENTS, P.O. Box 721, Uhrichsville, Ohio 44683
or sign up at **WWW.HEARTSONGPRESENTS.COM**